D1328311

Christmas on Ladybug Farm
with
Recipes from Ladybug Farm

Center Point
Large Print

Also by Donna Ball and available from
Center Point Large Print:

Vintage Ladybug Farm

**This Large Print Book carries the
Seal of Approval of N.A.V.H.**

Christmas on Ladybug Farm

with

Recipes from Ladybug Farm

— A Companion Cookbook —

Donna Ball

CENTER POINT LARGE PRINT
THORNDIKE, MAINE

ISBN: 978-1-61173-941-1

Library of Congress Cataloging-in-Publication Data

Ball, Donna.
  Christmas on Ladybug Farm with recipes from Ladybug Farm /
    Donna Ball.
    pages cm
  ISBN 978-1-61173-941-1 (library binding : alk. paper)
  1. Female friendship—Fiction.
      2. Farmhouses—Conservation and restoration—Fiction.
      3. Shenandoah River Valley (Va. and W. Va.)—Fiction.
      4. Christmas stories. 5. Domestic fiction. 6. Large type books.
      I. Title.
  PS3552.A4545C48 2013
  813'.54—dc23
                                                    2013029098

Christmas on Ladybug Farm

Chapter One

In Which Everything is Picture Perfect

Ladybug Farm was ready for Christmas. Two perfectly conical potted hemlocks flanked the bottom of the wide steps that led to the porch, each one decorated with hundreds of miniature red birds, tiny red bows, garlands of white beads, and white lights. The porch columns were wrapped in greenery and white lights, each one set off with a wreath stylishly decorated with silver glass balls and big red bows. The front door was draped with a swag of cedar into which sprigs of red-berried holly and white lights were cleverly woven, and on either side of it was a stack of gaily wrapped boxes, each topped with a giant red velvet bow. A huge wreath, decorated with shiny ornaments and silver and gold ribbon, adorned the front door.

Three rocking chairs were arranged in front of the door. Bridget, Cici, and Lindsay, each wearing fur-lined Santa hats and white sweaters, sat in the chairs, smiling fixedly at the blinking red light on the camera. Cici's daughter Lori knelt in front of them in a red ski vest and fleece lined boots, while seventeen year old Noah stood behind them in a heavy fisherman's knit sweater, one hand on

Lindsay's chair and the other on Cici's as he had been instructed, grimly staring down the camera.

"I'm melting," he muttered.

"My hair is as big as Dolly Parton's," Lori complained.

"I swear if that flash doesn't go off in the next second I'm going to burst into flames," Lindsay said.

Bridget said through clenched, smiling teeth, "Three . . . two . . . one."

The camera clicked just as Noah blinked, Lori wiped a drop of sweat from her nose, and Lindsay tugged the neck of her sweater away from her skin. Bridget got up to check the digital display and said, "Okay, one more time."

A chorus of groans was her only reply. Noah walked away, stripping his sweater over his head. Lori stood up. "I'm going to take a shower."

Lindsay moved for the door. "I'm going to put on my shorts."

Cici dragged off her Santa hat, twisted her hair into a ponytail and snapped it back with an elastic band. "Hold it," she commanded grimly.

Steps halted, shoulders slumped, and each of them turned reluctantly back. "What's the big deal about getting the Christmas picture done now?" Noah demanded, scowling. "You already sent out the Christmas cards."

"We always take the picture for next year's Christmas card this Christmas," Cici explained patiently. "That way we don't have to decorate the house for Christmas in the middle of the summer, just to get a photograph."

"Might as well *be* the middle of the summer," Lori complained. "If I'd wanted to spend Christmas in a sauna I could have gone to Mexico with Dad."

"This cedar is starting to look a little sad," said Bridget worriedly, rubbing a section of the door garland between her fingers. "Do you think we should make another one?"

"Seriously," Lindsay said, holding her sweater away from her neck and fanning the exposed skin. "Flames."

"Hottest December I ever do recall." Ida Mae pushed open the screen door with a tray of iced tea in her hands, and everyone rushed to grab a glass. "Radio says it's going to hit eighty-eight today."

The chorus of groans was punctuated only by gulps of iced tea. "How can it be eighty-eight degrees on Christmas Eve?" Lori demanded, pushing back her damp copper curls from her forehead. Her makeup had long since melted away, leaving nothing but an over-heated flush on her cheeks. "How *can* it?"

Bridget said, "Ida Mae, it must be a hundred and twenty degrees in that kitchen. Sit down, won't you, and try to cool off." She took the tray from her and set it on the white wicker table by the porch railing, nudging aside a candle-and-evergreen centerpiece to make room.

Ida Mae, who was somewhere between seventy and a hundred years old, had been keeping house at Ladybug Farm since long before Cici, Bridget and Lindsay moved in and called it home. Her iron gray curls were dark with sweat and, in deference to the heat, her customary attire had been lightened by several layers to include only a pair of faded, elastic-waisted denim pants, a print cotton dress topped by a man's Oxford cloth shirt, and a flour-dusted apron with a snowman on it. Her customary steel-toed work boots had been replaced, astonishingly, by a pair of red Crocs worn over argyle socks. She said, "Don't mind if I do," and lowered herself to the rocking chair Bridget had vacated, fanning her face with one of the starched cloth napkins from the tray. "But I can't let my yeast rolls sit too long in this heat. They'll rise up the size of pumpkins."

"I mean," insisted Lori, "this is *Virginia*. Didn't a whole colony freeze to death here one winter? How can it be eighty-eight degrees?" She said it as though her outrage could somehow provoke the weather gods into lowering the temperature. "Virginia!"

"It sure doesn't feel much like Christmas," Lindsay agreed, draining her glass. She wound her own shoulder-length auburn hair into a knot and stuffed it under her Santa hat. In another second, she jerked the Santa hat off and started fanning herself with it. She poured another glass of tea.

"Not like the first Christmas we spent here," Cici agreed, and for a moment she, Bridget and Lindsay shared a smile that was both rueful and nostalgic. "Speaking of almost freezing to death . . ."

The three friends had discovered the stately, if somewhat age-worn, mansion in the Shenandoah Valley by accident and had fallen quite hopelessly in love with its elegant charm and sweeping pastoral views. On an impulse they had decided to pool their resources, leave the suburbs, and purchase the house. They had spent the first year restoring the blowsy gardens and crumbling fountains, painting porches, refinishing the wide plank floors. They redecorated the enormous, sunfilled bedrooms and reclaimed the antique porcelain fixtures in the five bathrooms. And as they discovered and restored more of the old house's former glory, they had also discovered a new community, a new home, and a new family. Cici's daughter Lori had come to live with them at the end of that first year, and Noah had joined the family shortly afterwards. They had faced their share of challenges, but they had faced them together, and they knew they were here to stay.

"The Storm of the Century," Bridget said, and her smile faded into a shiver of reminiscent

11

horror as she remembered. "Boy, were we stupid."

Cici's eyebrows shot up into her honey-colored bangs. "Excuse me? You're the one who went out into a blizzard chasing after a dog!"

"Rebel," exclaimed Bridget, setting her glass on the railing with a clack. "He has to be in the photograph!"

"Are you kidding me? That dog is crazy!" This was from Lindsay. "Do you remember what happened last year when we tried to take his picture?"

Rebel was a working dog who determinedly resisted every effort to turn him into a pet. He had ostensibly been acquired to handle the flock of sheep that had come with the property, and he did that job extraordinarily well. Unfortunately, he considered every other moving object on the farm his responsibility to discipline as well, and he herded humans with the same ferocity that he directed toward the sheep. Bridget absently rubbed the indented scar on her arm that had been left by the border collie, and she didn't look so eager to find Rebel anymore.

"Hey, if the dog is going to be on the card, then Bambi should be," Noah insisted. "He's as much a part of the family as that dumb dog."

Bambi had followed Lindsay home from a walk when he was only a fawn, and Noah had adopted him. Now a full grown deer with the beginnings of an impressive rack, he roamed the farm's sixteen acres with the imperious fearlessness of one who knew exactly where he belonged.

"Bambi," Lori replied, staring at him, "is a deer. A wild animal."

He returned her stare belligerently. "You never heard of a reindeer? He's got a lot more reason to be on the card than a stupid dog."

Cici grinned and sipped her tea. "He's got a point. We could wind twinkle lights and garland around Bambi's antlers and put a big red bow around his neck."

Ida Mae stopped rocking. "You ain't bringing that wild animal up on my clean porch!"

"Are we gonna do this thing or not?" Noah said. "I need to go to town."

Lori stared at him incredulously. "You haven't done your Christmas shopping yet?"

He scowled at her.

Cici set down her glass with a sigh. "Okay, he's right, we all have a lot to do before the party tomorrow. Let's get this thing shot."

Bridget said, "I'll get—"

"No dog," Cici said firmly, "no deer. Where's my lipstick?"

"Where's my hairbrush?" Lindsay said. "Noah, put your sweater back on. And try smiling this time, will you?"

Lori picked up a hand mirror and gazed at her twenty-two year old face critically. "I look like a plague victim. Mom, you know it's really stupid to take these pictures a year in advance. I mean, next year we're not even going to look like this."

"I am," replied Cici indignantly, and slapped a tube of lipstick into her daughter's outstretched hand.

"You know what I mean." Lori's words were slightly muffled by the *O* she made of her mouth while she traced the perfect line of color around her lips, then filled it in with artistic strokes. "Last year Noah wasn't even in the picture. Next year who knows where I'll be?" She completed her lipstick, smacked her lips together, and admired the results in the mirror. "It's Whiskers all over again."

Lindsay, Bridget and Cici were deliberately silent. Noah opened his mouth to ask, "Who is—?" but the warning blaze in Cici's eyes cut him off in mid-breath.

Ida Mae pushed herself to her feet. "Well, I got a ham in the oven."

"Oh, Ida Mae, you should be in the photo!" Bridget said. "You're family, too."

Ida Mae gave her a look that suggested Bridget had clearly lost her mind. "You might have time for this foolishnesss," she said flatly. "I don't. Bring that tray in when you're done."

She let the screen door slam loudly behind her as she returned to the house.

Noah said, "Well, if she doesn't have to be in it, I don't see why I—"

"Put on your sweater," Lindsay snapped.

And Lori added, "Yeah, are you a part of this family or not?"

Cici said sharply, "Lori, mind your own business."

Bridget set the camera timer and said brightly, "Okay, everyone, twenty seconds!"

Noah pulled on his sweater and scowled into the camera. Lindsay pulled her Santa hat down over her ears. Bridget hurried into her chair, breathless. Lori declared, "Everybody, say 'peaches'."

Cici stared at her. "Peaches?"

Noah grumbled, "I'm not saying 'peaches'."

Lindsay twisted around to look at him. "Will you stop being so difficult? It's Christmas, for heaven's sake! Do what you're told!"

Bridget patted her short platinum bob a little frantically. "My hat!"

The camera clicked.

Lori smiled. "Peaches," she said.

Noah rolled his eyes and stalked away. Everyone else was absolutely silent. Then Bridget forced another, rather weak smile. "Okay, maybe just one more . . ."

"No!"

"No way!"

"I'm outta here."

The screen door slammed behind Noah and they could hear him clattering up the staircase to his room before even one of them could draw a breath to stop him.

"I promised to drive Ida Mae to deliver her fruitcakes," Lori said, scrambling to her feet. "I'd better go see what time she wants to leave."

And even Cici admitted, wiping her forehead with her Santa hat, "Maybe we can try again this evening, when it's cooler."

Lindsay grabbed a handful of ice from her glass and massaged her throat with it. "Who even cares? Why can't we just skip Christmas this year?"

Bridget stared at her. "Are you delirious?"

"I think that's a great idea," Cici replied a little irritably. "Let's just toss out twenty-five pounds of ham and turkey, a hundred and fifty cheese puffs, four pies, two cakes and three cases of wine—"

"I'll drink the wine," Lindsay objected.

Cici ignored her. "And let's just call all our neighbors and friends and tell them to stay home this year because it's too hot and we're not in the mood. All in favor, say Aye."

Bridget sighed as she started to dismantle the camera from the tripod. "Well, to tell the truth, except for the part about throwing out twenty-five pounds of ham and turkey, I could almost get on board with that right now."

"Ha." Lindsay tried for a note of smugness but

it came out as merely exhausted. "I knew there was a real person behind that perky little elf."

Lori widened her eyes meaningfully. "You people are horrible," she declared. "Where's your Christmas spirit?"

"Hey kid, guess what?" her mother said, sprawling out in the rocking chair and leaning her head against the back. "There's no such thing as Santa Claus."

Lori gave her a pitying look. "Too late, Mom. You already shattered all my illusions fifteen years ago with Whiskers."

All three women groaned.

"Exactly my point," said Cici. "You try to do something nice for someone . . ."

"Bah, humbug," said Lori, jerking open the screen door. "If you need me I'll be delivering fruitcakes, or caroling to prisoners, or reading to the blind, or—or something!"

Cici lifted a hand in weak salute. "That's my girl."

"Seriously," Lindsay said. She rubbed the last few remaining ice cubes over her face. "Don't you think Christmas would be a lot more fun if we only had it every four years, like the Olympics?"

"You have a point." Cici refilled her glass and Lindsay's with iced tea from the pitcher. "As much as I hate to admit it, it seems like we just get over one Christmas before it's time to start decorating for the next one."

She held the iced tea pitcher questioningly to Bridget, who shook her head. "That's because the planet is spinning faster," Bridget observed sagely. She snapped the locks on the tripod and set it beside the door, then started gathering the Santa hats. "It's all the earthquakes."

Lindsay shook the melted ice off her fingers and picked up her glass, leveling a look on Bridget. Cici paused to stare at her before resuming her chair, but both women were too wise to ask for details. Bridget ignored them and added, "It's true. Time is speeding up. I read it on the internet."

"Oh, well, if you read it on the internet," Cici said, and started rocking again.

"Great," muttered Lindsay. "Winters are getting hotter and time is getting shorter. Is it too much to ask to grow old on the same planet you were born on?"

"Come on, girls, this isn't like us." Bridget stacked the hats on the tea tray, took up her glass, and sank into her rocker. "We love the holidays, remember? Where is your Christmas spirit?"

"The North Pole?" suggested Lindsay.

Cici sipped her tea wearily. "I don't know," she said. "Maybe by the time you've seen as many Christmases as we have, it's hard to keep getting excited about it."

Bridget gave her a stern look. "How old *are*

you, anyway?" She pressed the cool glass of tea against her flushed face.

"The problem is that there aren't any children in the house," Cici said. "Little ones, I mean. Christmas is all about the children."

"The problem is that it's eighty-eight degrees in Virginia on Christmas Eve," returned Lindsay shortly. "The only thing children would add to that is sweat and sticky fingers. Not that I don't love your grandkids," she added hastily to Bridget. "Sorry they couldn't make it this year."

Cici smothered a grin in her glass, and Bridget just shrugged. "That's okay. I'd love to see them, of course, but kids today just don't appreciate Christmas like we used to. For them it's all about the Wii and the PlayStation, and grandparents don't have to be there for that. As long as UPS doesn't go on strike, they're good." She smiled and sipped her tea. "I'll never forget Christmas with my grandma in Atlanta. It wasn't just a day, it was a ritual. An event. And it started long before Christmas, with a trip downtown to have lunch at Rich's Tea Room and ride the Pink Pig."

"Ride the what?" Lindsay choked a little on her tea.

"Did you say pig?" Cici leaned forward in her rocker to stare at her. "And I thought I had an interesting childhood."

"Oh, come on." Bridget's tone was scoffing. "Everyone who so much as passed through

Atlanta in the sixties knew about the Pink Pig. It was a tradition. More than a tradition. A rite of passage."

"Okay," said Cici, watching her, "we've got silver to polish and floors to wax and presents to wrap, but this is one story I have got to hear."

Lindsay grabbed a Santa hat from the tray and started fanning herself with it again. "Can I listen to it in my bra and panties?"

Bridget slanted her an admonishing look. "It's not that kind of story."

Lindsay rolled her sweater up above her midriff and stretched out in the chair, fanning her bare stomach. A look of cautious relief came over her face. "Ah," she said, closing her eyes. "Pigs. Tradition. Tea room. Right."

Bridget said, "I really should help Ida Mae in the kitchen. I feel guilty letting her work so hard in this heat."

"If she wanted help, she'd ask for it," Cici said firmly, "and you're not leaving this porch until I hear about the pink pig."

Bridget smiled a little into her tea. "Well, okay. It really is a special Christmas memory for me. We used to go every year, my grandmother and me, from the time I was three or four. But it's the last time we went that I remember most. That was the year I found out my great-great-grandmother was a spy, and I became a thief."

Chapter Two

Ghosts of Christmas Past: Bridget

My grandmother was the last of the southern belles. She had lived in Atlanta all her life, and remembered when Peachtree Street was a two lane road lined with real trees. She never left the house without three things: a hat, a pair of gloves, and a girdle. She still referred to the Civil War as "the late unpleasantness" or "the War of Northern Aggression" and until the day she died she would not sit down at the table with a Yankee. I swear. I couldn't make that up.

She had a big Georgian-style brick house with a bay window right in front where she would put the Christmas tree every year. Oh my, it was a gorgeous thing—ten feet tall and covered with those big old fashioned colored lights and an absolute curtain of tinsel. There were hundreds of glass balls, and every child and grandchild had an ornament especially made just for him or her. My cousin had a pair of ballet slippers, because she was a dancer, and my uncle had an open Bible with gold writing on it, because he was a preacher. Mine was a crown with rhinestones, because Daddy always called me his princess. Traffic would slow down in front of Grandma's house, her Christmas tree in that window was so pretty. And her house smelled like cinnamon, oranges and evergreen the whole month of December.

Of course Christmas at Grandma's was a huge event, with all the aunts and uncles and cousins and in-laws, the good china and heavy silver even at the children's table, and so much food it looked like—well, it looked like Christmas at Ladybug Farm! But the best thing Grandma did every year was to take each granddaughter out to a special lunch, all by herself. And if you were under twelve, that could only mean one thing.

Rich's Department Store was a landmark in Atlanta, and every holiday season they would run a tram ride for kids with the car shaped like—you guessed it—a pink pig. The ride went around the building and above the street, and it was really pretty exciting for the little kids. But as you got older, the real thrill was the other part of the tradition—getting all dressed up in your Christmas velvet, knee socks and black patent Mary Janes, putting on your rabbit-fur head band and your little white gloves, and going downtown to Rich's tearoom to have lunch with Grandma.

Grandma always dressed up when she went downtown. That was part of the times, I think, and partly just the way she was raised. For our lunch that day she wore silk stockings and polished black pumps that matched her handbag, and a green silk brocade suit with a mink collar. She always let me help her pick out her jewelry, because a lady was not completely dressed until she put on her earrings, you know. And what a treat that was for me! Grandma's jewelry box was a treasure chest in every sense of the word. It was this big polished mahogany box that sat on top of her dressing table, and locked with a brass key. It opened into four or five tiers and each tier was lined with blue velvet and divided into sections for rings, earrings, necklaces and bracelets. My favorite was an amethyst ring in an old fashioned silver setting with so many intricate filigrees and curly-ques that it was impossible to clean. The design was black with tarnish in the center, and I thought it had been painted that way.

Every year while she was putting on her earrings, Grandma would let me wear the ring. This year when I slipped it on my finger, it actually fit! Well, almost anyway. When I showed her, Grandma laughed and said, "Well, that settles it then. This ring will be yours some day." Then she added, "Ladies' fingers were much smaller back in the day when this ring was made, you know. Imagine a grown up married woman with a hand as tiny as yours!"

I admired the ring on my finger and asked, "Which grown up married woman, Grandma?"

"That ring belonged to my grandmother, Ivy

Bodine Winchester, and she was a spy during the War of Northern Aggression."

Imagine, my great-great-grandmother a spy! I didn't even know that women could be spies, especially a woman as ladylike as I was sure anyone who was related to my grandmother must surely have been. Remember, this was a time in which I had never even heard of a woman doctor, much less a woman spy. It sounded like science fiction to me.

"How did she do that?" I asked, big-eyed.

"It was really very clever." Grandma carefully fastened one of the emerald earrings onto her lobe, watching herself in the mirror. "She volunteered at the mission hospital that treated Union soldiers . . . and also at the hospital that cared for our own gallant men. The Yankee soldiers were so grateful for the compassionate nursing of a gentlewoman that they often told her more than they should, and my grandmother had no compunction about passing along that information to certain Confederate wounded who were cleared to go back to the front. One time she made friends with the aide to a Yankee major and found out the troop position for the Battle of Kennesaw. She passed the information to a handsome captain who was recuperating from a shoulder wound, and he took the information back to save his whole battalion. After the war he came back to Atlanta and looked her up." She smiled. "He ended up asking her to marry him, and he gave her this ring."

I gazed in absolute rapture at the purple stone glittering on my finger, feeling as though I had been transported through the magic of the ring into a fairy tale. "Wow," I said.

She turned from the mirror, beautifully coiffed, exquisitely jeweled, and smiled at me. "Wow, indeed," she said. "The moral of the story, young lady, is that you can be anything you want to be. Greatness is in your heritage. Now," she said briskly, "get your coat and your gloves. It's rude to be late for lunch."

I hurried to put on my coat and gloves, but I didn't take off the ring, and Grandma didn't notice. Oh, I don't mean to pretend I forgot. I did it on purpose. I held on to it like a talisman, a magical gateway between the past and the future, because I wanted to believe it was mine, even though I knew it wasn't.

All through the bus ride downtown I could feel that ring on my finger beneath my glove, solid and warm, like something alive. We walked down the street to Rich's past the street corner Santas ringing their bells and past the giant Christmas tree with its miles of garland and ornaments as big as beach balls. The store was decorated like a winter wonderland and every inch of it smelled like Christmas. Rich's had the best Santa in town, with a real beard down to his chest, and real rosy cheeks, not painted on. I stood in line with Grandma and when it was my turn you can guess what I told him I wanted for Christmas: an amethyst ring.

There was nothing more elegant than the Rich's tearoom. I walked like a queen with my grandmother to our table with its heavy white tablecloth and napkins, and I sat with straight shoulders, like a real lady, and ordered a lobster salad, just like Grandma did. There was a giant Christmas tree in the corner decorated in blue and white, and a man at the grand piano playing Christmas carols. For dessert we had petit-fours with perfect little Christmas trees in the icing, and cups of hot chocolate topped with whipped cream and cinnamon. It was the most wonderful lunch I had ever had.

We rode the elevator to the rooftop and the Pink Pig. I tell you, I was on top of the world when I got on that ride. And when I got off it, I realized the amethyst ring was gone.

I don't know how it happened. I remembered the feel of it on my finger during the bus ride, and the sparkle of it on my finger at Grandma's house while I listened to the story of my courageous ancestor the spy. I remembered taking off my gloves at lunch. Frantically, I searched my pockets and shook out my gloves. It wasn't there.

I had no choice but to tell Grandma. I had stolen her ring, and lost it. I was so ashamed and miserable I could have died. But she just listened to me, gave one of those brisk nods of hers, and said, "Well, we'd best find it then, hadn't we?"

I wish you could have seen her. She insisted that the entire ride be stopped and every seat searched, and you know what? No one questioned her. We went back to the tearoom and she had the maitre d' search every square inch of the restaurant, and he was happy to do it for her. I had always thought of my grandmother as elegant and beautiful but I don't think I'd ever realized what a powerful woman she was. She didn't give orders, she never raised her voice, but the Queen of England couldn't have commanded more respect than she did. All she had to do was ask, in that gentle Southern drawl of hers, and suddenly fifteen or twenty people were scurrying around trying to make her happy. She never once did or said anything to make me think she blamed me, and she never let me see the disappointment she must have felt. She didn't have to, of course. I was disappointed enough in myself for both of us. And I couldn't bear to think about what my mother would say when she found out what I'd done.

But my grandmother never told her. We didn't find the ring, despite all those people searching for it. I might have been young, but I knew what irreplaceable meant, and I knew how valuable something that old must have been. I just wanted

27

to die. And I think Grandma knew I was punishing myself more than any adult could have done, because she said on the bus ride home, "Let's just keep this between ourselves, shall we? After all, I said the ring belonged to you, and what you chose to do with it really is no one's business but your own."

That was the moment I understood something about my grandmother that I had never been able to put into words before: She was a lady, from the inside out. That was what gave her her power. A genuine lady was more than someone who wore gloves on the bus and knew which earrings went with which hat. It was more, even, than someone who could shut down the most popular ride in the city at Christmastime just by asking. A lady was someone who would do everything in her power to make certain everyone around her felt good about themselves, because when the people you love are happy, you are happy.

I had started out the morning with my head full of dreams about my heroic ancestress, the Confederate spy, and if you had asked me then I would have said there was nothing in the world I wanted more than to be like her. But by the time I kissed my grandmother good bye that afternoon, I knew who the real hero was. And that was when I decided what I wanted to be when I grew up: a lady.

Chapter Three

In Which There Are
a Few Complications

"That was the last Christmas we had with my grandmother," Bridget said. "She had a stroke the next summer and died at home. Of course, that made her Christmas gift to me all the more meaningful, but even if she had lived another twenty years, I would have treasured it the rest of my life."

"What did she give you?" Cici asked.

Bridget stretched out her hand to display a silver filigree ring with a small amethyst stone on her pinkie finger.

"You found it!" Lindsay exclaimed.

Bridget nodded. "One of the waiters at the restaurant turned it in, and of course the manager called my grandmother immediately. I couldn't believe she would give it to me after I had been so irresponsible. Heaven knows, if it was one of my grandchildren I'd certainly think twice. But it was like a secret promise between us, and I think she understood that I valued the secret even more than the ring. My mother thought it was costume jewelry; if she had known the truth she never would have let me keep it. I only wear it at Christmas, and every time I look at it I think about the courage of one southern lady, and the classiness of another."

Cici sipped her tea, nodding thoughtfully. "So there really was a pink pig."

Lindsay stood. "I have got to get out of these clothes."

"And I've got to get back to work." Cici finished off her tea and picked up the tray. She glanced at Bridget. "Are you coming, Bridget?"

Bridget seemed for a moment not to hear her, her expression absent as she turned the ring slowly on her finger. Then she smiled, and got up to follow the others inside.

Noah pushed open Lori's door and came inside. "Hey," he said.

Lori finished tying her sneaker, frowning at him. "You could knock every once in awhile, you know. And I don't have any money, if that's what you're looking for."

He leaned against the doorjamb, arms folded, his expression preoccupied. "You always have money."

"Not at Christmas I don't."

"Anyway, I've got my own money. I've got a job, remember? Unlike some people."

Lori's scowl deepened. "What do you want?"

"What did you get your mom for Christmas?"

She tied the other shoe. "She likes Shalimar," she said.

"Perfume? You got her perfume?"

"*Expensive* perfume," she clarified.

"That doesn't seem very. . . . I don't know. Personal."

"I didn't have time to knit her a scarf."

"Yeah, especially since you'd have to learn to knit first. What do you think she'd like?"

"Who? My mom?"

"No. You know." He shrugged one shoulder uncomfortably and jerked his head toward the front of the house. "Her."

He could have been referring to any of the four women downstairs, but Lori did not pretend to misunderstand. "You mean Aunt Lindsay," she said. "Your mom."

Again, he shrugged and looked a little embarrassed. "And don't say perfume. Perfume is stupid."

She got to her feet, catching her hair back at the nape with a scrunchie. "You're being awfully picky for a guy who waited 'til Christmas Eve to do his shopping. This isn't Charlottesville, you know. Nothing is going to be open in town. Why don't you give her one of your paintings? She'd love that."

"She sees my paintings every day. That's not for Christmas."

"Well, maybe jewelry then. Every woman likes jewelry."

"Maybe," he muttered, but looked unconvinced.

"And have the store gift wrap it. That always makes it look special."

"Maybe."

"You'll have to go to Staunton. And you can't borrow my car. I'm using it."

"Don't need it."

"Look," Lori said, "the important thing is that she knows you thought about her. That's all moms really want—to know you're thinking about them. Although," she added with a shrug, "like my mom always says, diamonds are nice, too."

He regarded her for another moment, expressionless, then pushed away from the door. "See ya."

He started down the stairs and Lori called after him, "You're going to have a hard time carrying my forty-two inch flat screen on the back of that motorcycle!"

The grand old house had been returned to the splendor of a Victorian Christmas for the traditional Christmas party that was scheduled the next day. Swags of evergreen and ribbon adorned every doorway and was wrapped around the stair rail. Each bathroom had its own Styrofoam Christmas tree covered with moss and decorated with bouquets of dried flowers. There was a massive Christmas tree in the parlor and another one on the second-floor landing, overlooking the foyer. Even the pots of the two big ferns that flanked the doorway were filled with shiny multicolored Christmas balls.

But Lindsay, the artist among them, always surveyed the interior with a critical eye.

"You know what's missing?" she said, not for the first time. "Mistletoe. We always have mistletoe."

"I told you, there wasn't any this year," Cici replied. "I sent Farley out looking for some but he said it had been too dry." Farley was their handyman and closest neighbor. There were not many things the ladies had not learned to do on their own, but when they did come up against something they couldn't handle, Farley was the one to call.

"Besides," added Bridget, "what do three middle-aged women living alone need with mistletoe?"

Lindsay returned an arch look. "Maybe *you*'re middle aged."

Lindsay started up the stairs just as Noah bounded down them, two at a time. "Back in a bit," he said, without pausing.

"You promised to sweep the walk," she reminded him, but was speaking to his back before all the words were out.

"And fix that string of lights the wind

knocked down!" Cici called as he blew past her.

"And I need you to help me hang some more garland!" Bridget said.

He threw up a hand without looking back. "Later!"

"Be back before lunch!" Lindsay called. "Don't forget we're having our family Christmas dinner tonight! And, hey!" She took a step down, raising her voice. "Keep an eye out for mistletoe!"

The screen door banged.

Cici opened the door and called after him, "Paul and Derrick are coming for lunch! Don't be late!"

The only reply was, after a moment's delay, the roaring of a motorcycle engine, followed by the frantic barking of Rebel the border collie as he chased the machine around the house and down the drive.

Lindsay leaned against the evergreen-draped banister and watched through the screen door as the motorcycle disappeared in a cloud of dust and Rebel came trotting back up the drive, tongue lolling, his job done. She looked troubled.

"I'm a lousy mother," she said.

"Welcome to the club," Bridget replied cheerfully. "Being lousy is part of the job description."

"No, I mean it. I don't think Noah's happy with the way things have turned out."

"Don't be silly," Cici said, "of course he is. When we first met him he was a drop out camping in our back yard. Now he's got a scholarship to a private art school, he's on his way to college, and he's got you for a mother. Not to mention his own set of wheels. What's not to be happy about?"

Lindsay shook her head slowly. "I think he liked it better when I was just his teacher and he worked here. He knew where he stood then. I know legally adopting him was the best thing to do, for all sorts of reasons, but it changed everything. He doesn't even know what to call me."

"Well," Bridget reminded her, "he is seventeen years old, and that's practically an adult in his eyes. Maybe he thinks he's too old to have a mother. I know that's what my Kevin thought when he was that age, and I gave birth to him."

"Maybe that's the problem," Lindsay said unhappily. "Maybe he is too old to need a mother. And I'm too old to be one."

"Did you ever tell him what to call you?" Cici asked, practically.

"No," Lindsay admitted. "It never seemed appropriate. Besides, that's not the point. I don't care what he calls me. I just want him to feel comfortable here, like part of the family. To be happy."

"What do kids know about happy?" Cici shrugged.

"It's his first Christmas with a new mom," Bridget added. "Give him a chance."

Lindsay sighed. "Why does everything have to

be so complicated?" she said, and started up the stairs. "And *hot?*" Impatiently, she tugged her sweater over her head and unzipped her jeans.

Lori, passing her on the stairs, lifted an eyebrow. "Laundry day?" she inquired when she reached her mother.

Ida Mae came out of the kitchen in time to see Lindsay marching up the stairs in her bra, and gave a disapproving shake of her head. "That girl has got to get herself some hormones," she said. She wiped her hands on her apron and turned to Lori. "Well, come on then, let's get them fruitcakes loaded up if we're gonna get them all delivered before Christmas."

"How long have you been taking fruitcakes to people for Christmas, Ida Mae?" Lori asked as she followed her back through the kitchen toward the cold pantry.

"Too many years," replied Ida Mae. "That's the trouble with doing stuff for folks. They start expectin' it."

"Why did you start doing it, then?"

"I didn't. Miss Emily did."

"The woman who used to own this house?"

"That's right."

"That's her cookbook that Aunt Bridget is always looking at, isn't it? Is the recipe for the fruitcake in there?"

"You don't need a recipe for fruitcake. You just make it."

"Everything has a recipe," Lori replied. "Cooking is all chemistry, you know."

Ida Mae gave her a disparaging look. "How many recipes have you followed, girl?"

"Well . . . a lot," she admitted.

"And have you ever made anything worth eating?"

Lori's shoulders slumped. Despite both Bridget's and Ida Mae's diligent efforts, all concerned had finally been persuaded that the one thing Lori would never master was the art of cooking.

"Grab a basket off the wall there," Ida Mae advised as they moved down the short hall to the pantry. "That way we don't have to—"

She stopped in mid-sentence when she opened the pantry door, and stood stock still. Lori wrinkled her nose. "What is that smell?"

The cold pantry had been built to store non-perishable food items in a time when super-markets were not around every corner, and when a simple dinner party might mean a six course meal for thirty people. It was located on the north side of the house to remain cool in the summer, and lined with thick stone walls to keep the contents from freezing in the winter. There were bins to store things like potatoes and grains, and every wall was lined with shelves. Most of the shelves contained sparkling jars of jams and preserves that the women had put up during the summer, but from Thanksgiving until Christmas everything else was moved aside to make room for Ida Mae's fruitcakes.

"It smells like a distillery gone bad in here." Lori took a cautious step inside, her face screwed up. "Rotten fruit and booze. Is it supposed to smell like that?"

Ida Mae strode into the room and jerked the cord on the light bulb that was suspended from the ceiling. She took down one of the cheesecloth-wrapped packages that lined the shelves and stripped away the layers of brandy-soaked cloth until the delicacy inside was revealed. "Mold!" she exclaimed, and tossed the fruitcake onto the butcher block table in disgust. "My fruitcake's got mold on it!"

"How can anything get moldy with all that booze?" Lori asked, still wrinkling her nose, but Ida Mae ignored her, pulling down another cake and unwrapping it. That one, too was tossed onto the table.

One after another the cakes were stripped and tossed onto the table, and the outraged disbelief in Ida Mae's face grew. "They're spoiled! Ever' blamed one of them, spoiled!"

She turned on Lori. "It's your fault, all of you! Coming in here, messing with the way things are done, drinking up all my wine—"

Lori looked indignant. "I didn't drink your wine!"

"And then saying, 'Don't you worry, brandy will do just fine.' Brandy! Whoever heard of brandy on my fruitcake!"

Lori picked up a Mason jar half filled with a pale liquid and removed the lid, sniffing cautiously. She blinked and winced. "I think they meant *real* brandy," she said. "Not homemade." She sniffed again. "What is this, peach? It's awfully fruity."

Ida Mae snatched the jar from her and screwed the lid back on.

Lori glanced around. "How long has it been since you checked on them?"

"You soak them once a week," Ida Mae said, placing the jar on a high shelf. "That's how you make sure the cakes don't dry out. I was back here last Sunday."

"Well, that's got to be it then. The heat wave didn't start until this week. I think it just got too hot in here, and with all that fruit and sugar . . . well, those cakes were a Petri dish just waiting for a bacterium."

Ida Mae glared at her and Lori shrugged. "Chemistry."

Ida Mae turned back to the moldy fruitcakes that were discarded on the table, hands on hips. It was difficult to read the emotions behind the tightly compressed lips, but she was not a woman to waste time feeling sorry for herself. "Well don't just stand there," she told Lori. "Get me a trash bag from the kitchen and let's get this mess cleaned up."

When Lori returned with an oversized plastic garbage bag, Ida Mae was in the process of unwrapping and examining each cake one more time, just to make sure. One by one, they each were dropped into the bag. "Sixty-four years," she muttered. "Sixty-four years and never once did I miss a Christmas. Not even when Miss Emily died. Preacher Winston, Doc Emory, that old coot Jake Hodges, toothless as a tadpole for twenty years but Law, does he look forward to his fruitcake . . . Ever' last one of the Pritchet children, and their families too. They'll think I up and died. Sixty-four years, never missed a Christmas."

Lori said, "Well . . . couldn't you make them something else?"

Ida Mae gave her a look that could have melted stone, and tossed the next cake into the bag with a particular viciousness.

Lori was undeterred. "I mean . . ." She looked around the pantry. "Look, we've got plenty of that candied fruit, and a whole bucket of walnuts and lots of flour and sugar . . . why don't you make fresh fruitcakes? They just wouldn't be as old, that's all."

This time Ida Mae didn't even bother to glare at her. "Child, if you had the sense God gave a goat you'd still come up lacking. Even if I didn't have a thing else in this world to do on Christmas Eve, and even if I was inclined to ruin my reputation by giving out Christmas fruitcakes without a bit of seasoning on them, it takes a good three or four hours for each cake to bake, not to mention the measuring and the beating and the chopping and the pouring."

"Well . . ." Again Lori looked around the pantry, thinking. "What about cookies?"

Another fruitcake hit the trash bag with a disheartening plop. "Folks is got more cookies than they can eat this time of year."

"Not fruitcake cookies," Lori insisted. "We've got all of the stuff, and they'd only take about an hour to bake. I could help," she volunteered eagerly.

Ida Mae scowled and tossed away another cake. "Fruitcake cookies. I never heard such foolishness. I'd be laughed outta this county."

"What about the preacher, and Doc Emory, and the Pritchet children? Would you rather have them think you're dead? Or worse, that you don't care about them?"

Ida Mae looked at her suspiciously, but Lori could tell the idea was beginning to take hold. "Where did you ever hear about such a thing as fruitcake cookies, anyhow?"

"I read a recipe online," Lori said. "I could go print it out for you." She dropped the bag and started to turn for the door, but Ida Mae stopped her.

"I ain't cooking nothing from no recipe, young lady," she said sharply, "in particular one that you pulled out of that computer of yours." She thrust the trash bag back into Lori's hands and ordered, "Now take this out back and put it in the bin. Make sure the lid's on tight so the 'coons don't get it."

Lori's face fell and she trudged toward the door, dragging the bag. "I was just trying to help."

"You can help by bringing in that candied fruit when you're done, and then get yourself busy chopping walnuts," Ida Mae said, pushing past her. "I'll go preheat the oven."

Lori broke into a grin and she hurried out the door, lugging the bagful of discarded fruitcakes behind her.

When she returned to the kitchen with her arms full of candied fruit and a zippered plastic bag of walnuts, Ida Mae had already cleared off the big center work island and set up the stand mixer. There was a pile of sifted flour on a sheet of parchment paper next to the mixer, to which Ida Mae was adding generous hand-measures of aromatic ground spices—ginger, cinnamon, nutmeg and allspice. Lori pulled up a stool on the opposite side of the island, knowing better than to get in Ida Mae's way while she was working, and she started chopping walnuts.

"How did you decide who to give the fruit-cakes to?" she asked.

"I didn't. Miss Emily did." She opened a stick of butter into the mixing bowl, thought about it, and added another.

"Miss Emily is dead, Ida Mae," Lori reminded her gently.

Ida Mae shot her a dark look. "You think I don't know that? And mind you check for shells before you put them nuts in the bowl." She cracked four eggs, fresh from their own hen house that morning, over the butter.

"What I mean is," Lori explained, "most of the people she used to give fruitcakes to have got to be dead too. So how do you decide?"

"Lord, child, can't you sit for one minute without talking a body's head off?" She added brown sugar straight from the bag to the butter and eggs.

"Well, I've just been trying to figure it out. Doc Emory and the preacher I can understand, but who are the Pritchets? And that toothless person? You had over twenty fruitcakes there. Who did all the rest go to?"

"God bless America," Ida Mae muttered, "I never did know a girl that could ask more questions. Every time you come home from that fancy school of yours I spend half my time explaining stuff to you that either ain't none of your business or you ought to be able to figure out for yourself."

Lori shrugged good naturedly. "I'm curious."

Ida Mae looked at her, lips pursed in disapproval. "If I tell you, will you let me have some peace? And watch out for them shells."

Lori grinned. "I *knew* there was a story."

Chapter Four

Ghosts of Christmas Past: Ida Mae

That first Christmas after the War was kind of a sad time around here. Miss Emily had lost her oldest son in the Pacific, and her youngest, that would be the judge only he wasn't the judge then, was still stationed overseas till his tour was up. My own Jackson, that's my husband may God rest his weary soul, was holed up in the VA in Norfolk with a shot up leg, and I couldn't stay up there with him because I didn't have the money, though I tried to get up there on weekends when I could. Miss Emily let me stay on here as long as I helped out with the house and cooking and such, though there wasn't that much to do with just the two of us.

So many of our boys didn't come home at all, and them that did were all broke up on the outside or all changed on the inside—kind of sad and empty and quiet like. Oh, I don't mean to say there wasn't a share of weddings and welcome-homes and church suppers when those troops came marching home, but there was an awful lot of empty places at the dinner table too.

Back during the war, Miss Emily ran a boarding house for soldiers' wives, you know, but now all the wives were gone back to their families, and this would be the first Christmas she'd be spending all alone. Miss Emily was one of them women that don't let on as to how she is inside, but I could tell it was breaking her up to think about that big old empty table come Christmas time. But like I said, she wasn't one to just sit back and let life beat her up, so she came up with the idea that we was to have a big old Christmas party, and invite everybody in the county. Why not? she figured. The war was over. It was time to celebrate.

Well, I was all for that, but I worried about my poor Jackson, and how I was going to get up to see him with all the extra work to do, and whether I'd be paid enough for a bus ticket to Norfolk for Christmas. I was knitting him a sweater, and I'd counted on giving it to him in person on Christmas day. But I didn't say anything to Miss Emily about that. It was so good to see her smiling again, and I didn't want to spoil it for her.

We started fixing and planning and cleaning and decorating right after Thanksgiving. First was the fruitcakes. We used up a whole summer's worth of dried apples and raisins and figs and brandied cherries, and then she'd boil down lemon and orange rinds in sugar until they were just like candy—that's what we did, you know, before we had all this fancy stuff in plastic boxes, and I'll tell you the truth, I don't know but what the old way wasn't better.

We piled up the whole table with flour and spices, and my, didn't this kitchen smell like heaven in a bowl! It took a whole jug of molasses and a pitcher of buttermilk fresh from the dairy. We shelled walnuts and pecans for days. We mixed up the batter with a big wooden spoon and baked the cakes in tube pans. We were doing nothing but fruitcakes from Monday to Wednesday, and I declare I'd never seen Miss Emily as happy as she was bustling back and forth in that kitchen, baking up a storm.

Now Miss Emily wasn't much of a drinker, but her son the judge, even though he wasn't a judge back then, he had brought back a case of wine from France when he was home on leave, and she figured that would be good enough to keep the cakes moist, so every week we'd go in the cold pantry and pour a little more wine on the cakes to keep them soaking. By the time the judge got home there wasn't a bottle left in that case, but that's a different story.

She sent out invitations to every family in town, from the mayor on down, on this thick cream colored paper with her initials engraved in the corner and stamped in gold on the envelope. We started sweeping out, and airing out, and washing down the windows with vinegar and polishing up the floors with turpentine and the furniture with beeswax, and we took down that big old chandelier and soaked every one of those crystals in soapy water. And let me tell you, I wasn't doing it all by myself, neither. Miss Emily tied up her hair in a rag and put on a dustcoat and was down on her knees scrubbing away just as pleased as she could be. We got some of the boys to cut down one of the big cedars out on the back lot, and we put it in the front parlor there by the big window, and decorated it up nine ways to Sunday. We sat in the conservatory there on the stone floor for days on end and twisted spruce branches into wreaths for every window in this house, fancying them up with dried flowers from the summer and oranges and apples from the root cellar, and while we worked, we talked. We got to be right good friends. I'll tell you the truth, though it shames me to say it, I started thinking it might not be such a bad thing to miss seeing the look on Jackson's face when I gave him his sweater, after all, if I could stay and see Miss Emily's party through.

It was the Friday before Christmas when we heard the civil defense siren go off. Now, you wouldn't know anything about that I reckon, but if you'd just lived through six years of a war, you better believe that sound could turn your bowels to water before you could take a breath. We used to have drills once a week before VE day, but it had been months since anybody'd heard that sound, and this weren't no drill. I recollect I was polishing up Miss Emily's fine Havilland soup tureen and I dropped it smack on the floor. It broke into fifteen separate pieces but she didn't say a word to me, she didn't even notice. She just looked at me with a face like parchment and eyes as big as moons, and I don't think she took a breath until that sound died down. I know I didn't. And I'll tell you the truth, seeing her that scared was almost worse than the thing that had scared us in the first place.

It was only a minute or two, but it was the longest minute of my life. That's how long it took Miss Emily to remember that the commissioners had decided that, since the war was over and they had this nice new siren with nothing to use it for, that they'd conscript the civil defense plan into a *county* defense plan, and use the siren in case there was to ever be a big emergency to call in the volunteer fire fighters and whatnot. So she went right to the phone and called the sheriff's department, and when she hung up the look in her eyes was almost more terrible than the one that had been there when we first heard that siren go off. But her shoulders were squared off and her mind was busy, dealing with what she had to deal with, like she always did.

"Ida Mae," she said, because she always called

me by my rightful name, "I want you to go upstairs and get every blanket you can find and put them in the boot of the Pontiac. Then fill some jugs with water and pack a basket full of that ham you made and the biscuits from breakfast. The boiler at the school just blew up. There were children inside."

Miss Emily ran around the house getting coats and packing jars of hot coffee in quilts and thinking about the things people might need like she always did, and I piled the blankets and the water and the food in the boot of the Pony and we took off. To this day I can't think about what we saw when we pulled up in the school yard without going all cold and shivery inside. It was a the last day of school before the holidays, don't you know, and there'd been a Christmas party, and near about every child in the county was there that day. Nine of them wouldn't live to see Christmas. Mary Pritchet, the third grade teacher, brought out twenty five of them alive, but she went back in one time too many and didn't come out again. I don't reckon there was one family in this county that wasn't standing in that school yard, wailing and praying or just staring and hoping, and Miss Emily and me, we did what we could, passing out food and blankets and coffee and water for those poor firemen, but it wasn't enough. It wasn't near enough.

It seemed like God had pure turned his back

on us that Christmas, it surely did. It wasn't enough that we had lost so many of our fine menfolk to the war, but now our children were gone too. It was a hard pill to swallow. Too hard. Miss Emily and me, we came home late that night bone weary and half-froze from standing out all day, our clothes splotched with water and our skin smudged with soot and our hair smelling like smoke and death, too tired and too hurt to do anything but sit in the dark in front of the fire and just rock. And then, after awhile, Miss Emily said, real quiet like, "Ida Mae, you and I are so lucky. Praise God, we are so lucky."

I thought about my Jackson all alone up in Norfolk with his shot up leg, and I thought about Miss Emily's oldest buried somewhere in Flanders, and I never thought either one of us would ever feel lucky, but I did that night. I felt like the luckiest woman God had ever made.

After all our hard work, there wasn't no Christmas party that year. On Christmas Eve, we wrapped up all those fruitcakes Miss Emily had meant to give to the dignitaries that came to her party, and we went around the countryside, stopping to leave one at the house of every family that had lost a child in the fire, or a son in the war. And then Miss Emily put a bus ticket in my hand and told me to go on, and spend Christmas with my loved one. I hated to leave her alone, but I couldn't bear to think of my Jackson all alone at Christmas in that hospital either. So I hugged her and I thanked her, and I grabbed my satchel and I got on that bus.

You won't believe what I found when I got to Norfolk and unpacked my satchel. It was two slices of Miss Emily's fruitcake, wrapped in paper and tucked down under Jackson's sweater. Jackson and I had it for dessert the next day after the hospital turkey dinner, and I want you to know, it was the best fruitcake I ever tasted.

And it was my best Christmas, too.

Chapter Five

In Which Christmas Falls From the Sky

Lori had stopped chopping walnuts, and her expression was somber. She said quietly, "Ida Mae, I never knew."

Ida Mae used a wooden spoon to fold in the dried and candied fruit, working the ingredients around the big yellow mixing bowl with all the vigor of a boxing champion at a sparring match. "It's not all Santy Claus and reindeer at Christmastime," she said without looking up from her work, "and Miss Emily thought it was important to keep that in mind. Every year, we'd remember the families that had lost a child with a special fruitcake at

Christmas. Sad to say, the list got longer every year. There was Korea, and Vietnam, and now them godforsaken countries in the desert. It's only right to do a little something extra to honor the empty plate at the Christmas table."

Lori surreptitiously blotted a corner of her eye with the back of her hand. "But Miss Emily's son, he did come back, right?"

"Of course he did. And I suwannee, was he mad about that case of wine we'd used up." There was the hint of a chuckle in her voice. "But that very year was when he started the vineyard, and it wasn't till we started using the Blackwell Farms wine to soak the fruitcakes that we became what you'd call legendary around here. Of course, after that first year, her Christmas parties was the hottest ticket in town. I wish you coulda seen this place, all done up like that castle in Asheville, what do you call it?"

"The Biltmore House?" suggested Lori.

She gave a sharp nod. "You about ready with them nuts?"

Lori scraped the contents of her cutting board into the bowl. Her voice, and her face, were touched with wonder. "Don't you think that's kind of weird—that now we're giving the same kind of Christmas party Miss Emily used to, and we didn't even know about it?"

"I do not," declared Ida Mae. "The house remembers, even if folks don't."

Lori sat back on her stool, looking puzzled and touched by the sentiment.

Ida Mae gave the wooden spoon two more turns around the bowl. "Well don't just sit there, girl, get out the baking sheets and start greasing them with butter. The day's half done and we'll be doing good to get these out before the reindeer fly as it is."

Lori said, "You know what would go really good in those cookies, Ida Mae?"

Ida Mae gave a derisive sniff. "Like I'd ever be listening to the likes of you on a recipe."

Lori said, "Some of that peach brandy."

Ida Mae looked at her, her brows drawn together in their usual scowl, her lips tight. And then, slowly, she smiled. "You know something, girl?" she said. "There might be hope for you yet."

"I told you we should have gotten new lights this year," Lindsay said. She stood back and surveyed the Christmas tree with her hands on her khaki-clad hips. Now barefoot, in cotton shorts and a halter top with her hair caught up in a pony tail, she was in a much better mood. "That's two strings that have gone out in the past week."

The Christmas tree was a nine-foot fir that dominated the spacious parlor and filled the entire room with the sweet smell of the green outdoors. It was wrapped in miles of multi-colored miniature lights and studded with the treasured ornaments of the ladies' three consolidated households—lace angels, gingerbread men, Santa faces with cotton beards, crystal unicorns, jewel-toned teardrops and spheres— along with a couple of hundred silver and gold glass balls in a myriad of sizes. Bridget had hung her treasured collection of antique Christmas cards by ivory ribbons from selected branches, and Lindsay had nestled a small, fluffy white teddy bear into the limbs. This year, for added panache, they had woven silver-blue and silver-pink ribbons in and out of the greenery, proving once and for all that there is no such thing as an over-decorated Christmas tree.

Bridget said, "There probably should be a rule. You know, like the one that says change your smoke detector batteries when you change the clocks for Daylight Savings Time. Some of these lights are twenty years old."

Lindsay gave her a dismissing look. "How can they be twenty years old? They weren't even making miniature lights twenty years ago."

"Sweetie, I don't know how to tell you this, but you're a lot older than you think."

Lindsay looked somewhat disturbed by that, and chose not to reply.

The base of the tree was already crowded with gaily wrapped presents, and Cici nudged these aside carefully as she wiggled under the tree, the plug from the final string of lights in hand. As she did, one of the lower limbs snagged her back pocket and the crystal angel atop the tree shimmied dangerously. Both Lindsay and Bridget lunged forward, hands outstretched protectively.

Cici plugged in the lights. "How's that?"

A cheer of approval went up.

"Perfect!"

"Good for you!"

Cici scooted back out from under the tree, brushing dead nettles from her hair. She had changed into a tank top and jeans, and the red marks of abrasive branches were evident on her freckled arms and chest. She had been working on the lights for half an hour.

"Okay," she declared, pushing a hand through her sweaty hair, "let's check the rest of them."

The Christmas decorating had been divided equitably. Bridget had been in charge of the mantel, which was draped in burgundy velvet and gold rope, accentuated by an antique mirror, an evergreen garland, and champagne glasses filled with miniature white lights. Lindsay had decorated every flat surface with bouquets of evergreen and red carnations, accessorized with red glass balls and twinkling white lights. A heavy garland of evergreen and white lights accentuated the entrance to the parlor, and wound its way up the banister to the landing, where another fully decorated Christmas tree looked down upon visitors from above. The three of them had wound evergreen, red ribbon and white lights around the porch columns, and fashioned wreaths for all of the front-facing windows, all interwoven with white lights. The doorway was draped with evergreen, red ribbons, and lights, as were the evergreens lining the walk. The porch roof line was swagged with ribbons, garlands and lights, but a brief windstorm two nights previously had knocked down the lights on the west side of the porch.

"You know," declared Bridget philosophically, "even if all the lights work perfectly today there's no guarantee they'll work tomorrow. I think Lindsay is right. We should have replaced the lights."

"Well we didn't. So let's just make the best of it and replace them next year, okay?"

Cici plugged in the mantel lights and the front porch lights and started toward the porch. "Somebody will have to hold the ladder while I try to get that string of lights tacked up again. I can't wait any longer for Noah to help. Where did he go, anyway?"

"Where he went was to my bad side," Lindsay muttered, following her. "You'd think after living here almost three years he'd know that the one day you do not want to blow off is the day before Christmas. It's all hands on deck, and he knows we were counting on him."

There was a sudden cacophony of barking from

the front yard and Bridget hurried to the door. "Oh, good, maybe he's back."

"I don't hear a motorcycle." Lindsay's tone was dark with skepticism and she frowned at her watch. "If he's hanging out with those boys at the pizza parlor again . . ."

"Speaking of pizza," Cici said, "are we going to have lunch? A ham sandwich or something?"

"It's not even eleven o'clock."

"Maybe, but breakfast was six hours ago and I've been smelling ham and turkey and sausage dressing and pecan pie for the past five of them, and I'm starved."

Bridget turned her head toward the kitchen. "Something does smell awfully good, doesn't it? I wonder what Ida Mae is baking."

Cici gave a curious tilt of her head. "Baking? I thought she'd gone with Lori to deliver her fruitcakes."

"I don't think so," Bridget said. "When I was back there to take the ham out of the oven Ida Mae was up to her elbows in flour and Lori was chopping something."

"Never a good sign," Cici murmured worriedly.

Lori chose that moment to come in from the kitchen, staggering a little under the weight of the huge picnic basket she carried in both hands, and declared happily, "Santa Claus is here! Or maybe I should say Santa Clauses. Uncle Derrick and Uncle Paul are coming up the driveway.

They're staying the night, right? Because Ida Mae is waiting for me in the car."

Paul and Derrick were not Lori's real uncles, any more than Bridget and Lindsay were her real aunts. The close friendship between all of them for almost thirty years had transcended a blood relationship and formed its own kind of family which, for Lori as well as everyone else, was just as genuine—and in some ways even more treasured—than the ties that bound them to the families into which they had been born.

"I thought you'd already left," Cici said, running her fingers through her hair and snagging a few more fir needles.

"Minor setback," replied Lori cheerfully.

Cici ran a disapproving gaze over her daughter's denim shorts, belly-skimming tank top and flip-flops. "You're not going out to deliver fruitcakes dressed like that, are you?"

"Nope." Lori nudged open the screen door with her hip and edged the basket through. She picked up a Santa hat from one of the rocking chairs and plopped it on her head, grinning at her mom. "Back in a flash."

"That's what Noah said two hours ago," Lindsay muttered.

The cacophony of barking grew louder as the Prius glided silently to a stop in front of the steps, and Lori took advantage of the border collie's frantic preoccupation to edge past him toward her own car. "Merry Christmas, Uncle Paul, Uncle Derrick!" she called on her way past them. "I'm off to play Lady Bountiful. What did you bring me?"

Paul opened the passenger door and used it as a shield between himself and the dog to call back, "Cashmere!"

"Yay!"

Derrick opened the driver's side door and added, "Diamonds!"

"Double Yay! Gotta run." This was no exaggeration, as Rebel, having tired of charging the car, suddenly pricked up his ears and turned toward her. Lori hurried toward the safety of her own car, the basket banging against her knees.

"I hope you brought cooler weather!" Cici declared as she skipped down the steps to greet them.

"I hope you brought rum," said Lindsay, right behind her.

Paul, a slim, salon-tanned man with perfectly coiffed silver hair and Ralph Lauren sunglasses, carefully checked for the whereabouts of the dog before emerging from behind the car door. He was wearing a tropical shirt, Bermuda shorts, and thong sandals, and Bridget laughed as she came down the steps behind the other two. "I thought you'd cancelled your trip to the Bahamas this year."

"Had too, darling. Too bloody hot." Derrick,

similarly attired, closed his own door and came around the car. "Fortunately, we didn't have to waste a perfectly good wardrobe."

They embraced all around, and the two men started unloading bags from the car. "Actually, I did get Lori a cashmere sweater," Paul confessed as he handed a double-handled Christmas bag filled with wrapped packages to Cici. "But in my defense, it was forty-two degrees when I bought it. Maybe she can exchange it for a bikini and a sunhat."

"Well, *I* brought rum," announced Derrick, passing an insulated cooler to Lindsay, "along with brandy, bourbon and all the fixings for my famous Southern Comfort eggnog—including, of course, Southern Comfort."

"God bless you!" Lindsay said, hugging the cooler to her chest. "I'll help you get it started."

"Let them unpack first, for heaven's sake." Bridget peeked inside the gourmet market bag Paul passed her. "Oh my goodness, is that white truffle oil? And Egyptian dates?"

"Unpacking can wait," Lindsay said, starting up the steps, "but the longer it takes to get this eggnog in the bowl, the less of it I get to drink. I'll meet you in the kitchen, Derrick."

"I guess I'd better hurry," Derrick said, and flung the strap of his leather duffle over his shoulder. "Where is Noah?"

"We think he may have forgotten that Christmas was on the twenty-fifth this year," Cici replied dryly. "He had a few last-minute errands."

"Don't hold it against him." Paul took the remaining bags in hand and started up the steps with Bridget and Cici. "He's a teenager. You're lucky he remembered what month it is. The place looks nice, by the way," he added. "Why are all the lights on?"

"We were testing them."

"You've got a string out."

"I know," Cici said. "You've been drafted to hold the ladder while I fix it."

Bridget opened the screen door and paused at the threshold, sniffing the air. "Do you smell something burning?"

Cici edged in beside her. "That's odd. You don't suppose Ida Mae went off and left something baking, do you?"

Bridget left the packages on the table by the door and moved toward the kitchen. "Lindsay, is something in the oven?"

Lindsay came from the kitchen, her nose wrinkling. "I smell something burning."

Bridget hurried past her to check for herself.

Paul glanced around, sniffing the air. "Did you light candles?"

Derrick came from behind Lindsay, uncapping a bottle of whiskey. "Has anyone seen the bag with the . . ." He stopped and turned his nose to the air, glancing around. "What's burning?"

Bridget came through the dining room, her face creased with anxiety. "Everything is off in the kitchen, and nothing is burned on the stove."

"It's not food," Derrick insisted. "It's more like candles."

"Actually," said Lindsay, "it's more like when Noah was burning the grass off around the vineyard last spring. It's like—"

"Oh my God." Cici gripped Paul's arm, staring with her expression frozen in horror up at the balcony. "It's the upstairs Christmas tree!"

Even as she spoke, the fine film of smoke that had hovered over the balcony drifted into a patch of sunlight and became clearly visible to all. Cici dashed toward the stairs and Bridget cried, "Cici, be careful!" but she was close behind. "Don't get burned!"

The tree was not yet blazing, but they both could clearly see the tendrils of smoke curling from its branches when they reached the balcony, and the pungence of evergreen was much stronger there. Cici lunged forward and Bridget caught her shirt. "You'll catch on fire!"

"Everything will catch on fire if we don't unplug those lights!"

Cici flung herself to the floor and yanked the plug from the wall, then quickly scooted back. "We need to wet it down," she said, gasping as she got to her feet and backed away. "It's going to go up any minute."

"You can't put water on an electrical fire!" Bridget said, coughing and waving at the smoke.

Derrick ran toward the stairs with the bottle in his hand, and Lindsay grabbed his arm. "Don't throw alcohol on it!"

"Are you insane? This bottle cost seventy-five dollars!" But he looked for a moment at a loss for what to do.

"The hose!" cried Paul, turning toward the door. "Where's your garden hose?"

"The outside water is turned off!" Lindsay raced to the cellar to turn on the valve while Paul and Derrick clattered down the front steps in search of the garden hose.

Cici whirled around, grabbed a vase full of evergreen and red carnations and tossed the contents on the tree. The Christmas tree, now dripping with red carnations, still smoked. She thrust the vase at Bridget and cried, "More water!" She ran back across the landing to her room and returned with an antique porcelain washbasin filled with water, sloshing most of it on the floor before she reached the tree. Bridget tossed another vase full of water on the branches and raced back to refill it.

Cici said, "We've got to get it away from the wall! That wallpaper will go up as fast as the pine branches do."

"Cici, don't get too close!" Bridget said.

"Hold on! We've got it! We're coming!"

63

Derrick and Paul burst through the front door like something out of a scene from a Ron Howard film, each of them holding a section of garden hose as they charged up the stairs. Cici grabbed a branch of the wet, smoking tree and dragged it away from the wall just as the length of the garden hose ran out, stopping Derrick's forward momentum abruptly three steps from the landing. Cici turned toward him and said, "Wait, I think—"

Just then the water came on full blast, spraying from the garden hose like a geyser that soaked Cici from head to foot, knocking her back into the tree. She sputtered and flailed for balance, and the tree, now leaning precariously against the railing, began to tip over. They all watched in helpless horror as it fell, with a steaming, sizzling crash, onto the floor below just as Lindsay came through the door from the cellar.

For a long moment no one said anything. Bridget and Cici moved to the railing and peered cautiously down at the disaster. Lindsay stood stock still, just staring. Water dripped from the landing and splashed into the puddle that was beginning to form on the polished floor around the tree.

Paul dragged his gaze away from the broken mass of damp evergreen and looked at Derrick without expression. "Remind me again," he said, "why we don't visit more often."

Bridget emptied the last dustpan of soggy evergreen needles and broken ornaments into the trash, Lindsay carried the last armload of wet towels to the laundry and Cici emptied out the bucket of sooty, soapy water into the yard. Paul returned from dragging the Christmas tree to the mulch pile behind the barn, brushing futilely at the stains and splotches on his shirt. Derrick wadded up the newspaper he had been using to clean the smoke off the windows and stuffed it into the kindling bin beside the fireplace.

Cici sank into her rocking chair. She had changed out of her soaked clothes into a fresh pair of shorts and a tee shirt with a picture of a dancing elf on it. Both were now smudged with sap and stained with sweat, and her hair, which she'd drawn up into a topknot to dry, was now straggling wetly over her cheeks. "The house still smells like a wet campfire," she said.

Paul sank down on the top step, leaning back against a pillar. "You could always light some candles."

"Very funny." Bridget sat down with a sigh. "Well, at least we can all relax now. It wouldn't be Christmas at Ladybug Farm without a disaster, and now we've had it. We're good for the duration."

"You're awfully optimistic," Lindsay said, "to limit our holiday luck to one disaster."

Paul said, "You know the best stories are always when things go wrong. And so are the best memories." He chuckled a little. "Cici, if you could have seen your face when the water came on."

She glared at him and he threw up his hands defensively. "Who knew the water pressure would be that high?"

Lindsay grinned. "You've got to admit, it was kind of funny. I mean, in retrospect. Now that the house didn't burn down or anything."

Cici turned on her, but her lips twitched with repressed mirth. "You should have seen *your* face when the Christmas tree fell from the sky and practically landed at your feet."

Lindsay started to giggle, and so did Cici, and then Bridget. Then Bridget sat forward, wiping her eyes, and placed her hands firmly on her knees. "Well, it's almost one and you all must be starved. I'll start lunch."

"Forget lunch," said Lindsay, and her laughter faded into a small groan, "what I need is a drink."

Perfectly on cue, Derrick pushed through the door with a tray in his hands. "Ladies," he announced, "it has to be five o'clock somewhere. Merry Christmas."

The tray contained five holly-patterned glasses filled with creamy eggnog, a plate of dates, cheeses, olives and crackers, and another plate of Christmas cookies. He set it on the table to a chorus of cheers and eager scrambling for glasses.

Lindsay took a sip and her eyes widened as she swallowed. "That," she pronounced, "is eggnog. If there were any justice in this world, you would be a god."

He inclined his head modestly. "I couldn't agree more."

Bridget took a sip. "If this isn't one of the seven deadly sins, it should be."

Cici tasted hers. "Oh, my," was all she said.

Paul lifted his glass. "To good stories," he said, "and great memories. There's never a shortage of either at Ladybug Farm."

"Hear, hear," replied Derrick. They all leaned forward to touch glasses, and they drank.

Cici leaned back in her rocking chair, laughing softly. The others looked at her. "Sorry," she said. "I can never drink eggnog without remembering my first Christmas as a married woman. Talk about disasters . . ."

A grin spread from Paul to Derrick to Bridget to Lindsay, and they all settled back, sipping eggnog and nibbling cookies, to listen.

Chapter Six

Ghosts of Christmas Past: Cici

Richard and I had only been married six months, and we were living in this awful little apartment just outside of D.C.—you know the kind with plywood cabinets and Formica countertops and a leaky toilet. You had to close the dishwasher to open the oven, and two people couldn't move past each other in the kitchen. It had olive green carpet and a burn mark on the fake-marble bathroom vanity in the shape of a cigarette. Our bed was a mattress and box spring on the floor, not because we didn't have a real bed frame but because if we set it up we wouldn't be able to open the bedroom door. The windows were these odd little slits that reminded me of gun ports. I tried to dress them up with curtains but that only made them look more ridiculous.

Richard was finishing up law school and I was working full time downtown with a consulting firm, so neither one of us had much time to spend on fixing up the place, or much energy left to even care, really. But then we got the word: Richard's parents were coming to town to spend Christmas with their only son and his new bride. You can just imagine how thrilled I was.

My mother-in-law was the most intimidating

person I'd ever met, and the only good thing about living in that hideous little apartment was that it was nine hundred miles away from her. She had a way of smiling at me that somehow made it abundantly clear I would never be good enough for her son, and she never gave a compliment without an edge. "Darling, what a sweet haircut. I'm sure it will grow out." Or, "I love your blouse, dear. It almost looks like real silk, doesn't it?" That kind of thing. Every time she hugged me I looked for a knife in her hand. And her husband wasn't much better. He chewed on a pipe—never lit it, mind you, just chewed on the stem—and spoke in grunts. The very thought of spending an entire Christmas with them gave me cold chills.

The good news was that there wasn't enough room in that apartment for a cat, much less two more adults, so they made reservations in a hotel. And Richard was a little too quick to promise me that we'd have Christmas dinner at a restaurant so I wouldn't have to worry about cooking, but it didn't take a genius to figure out that what he really wanted was to make sure I didn't embarrass him in front of his parents. Well, granted, between my job and Richard's crazy hours at school, I hadn't had a lot of time to practice my skills in the kitchen, but I took that as a personal challenge. I was not going to give Richard's mother one more reason to think I wasn't good enough for her son.

I was going to make them a Christmas dinner they'd never forget.

I spent practically my entire pay check on Christmas decorations. I made red velvet curtains for those awful little windows, and a red velvet runner for my white linen wedding tablecloth, and big red velvet bows for our garage-sale dining chairs. I got a four-foot Scotch pine from the lot across the street, and by the time I got it set up in front of the window and decorated with twenty feet of red garland and five boxes of red glass balls, I have to admit that apartment looked almost pretty. Of course, you couldn't see the television and you had to crawl over the back of the sofa to get to the bathroom, but even Richard agreed it was worth it. We would sit on the sofa at night with all the lights off except the Christmas tree lights and snuggle and talk and let one thing lead to another, and it was definitely worth it.

The closer the big day came, the more determined I was to make this an event like no other. I started the countdown two weeks in advance. I drew up a flow chart. I sprayed pine boughs and holly sprigs with floor wax so they wouldn't dry out and bought up every red candle in town. The place started to look like a cathedral —or maybe a wedding chapel for woodland elves. Every time Richard came home he had to duck his head to avoid some new hanging evergreen spray or weave around a tower of peppermint candies. He was a good sport about it though. He knew as well as I did that the more bows and wreaths I hung, the less noticeable the stained walls and cracked tiles became.

The one thing Richard was not so supportive about was my cooking the entire meal from scratch. He kept bringing home deli fliers that advertised "complete Christmas dinner, fully prepared and delivered piping hot to your home" and he cut out menus that the local restaurants placed in the newspaper to advertise their Christmas dinner specials. I was undeterred. I started thawing the turkey three days in advance in the refrigerator, just like the package instructions advised. I made a batch of sausage cheese balls from the recipe on the back of the biscuit mix package and put them in the freezer, ready to pop into the oven half an hour before company arrived. I made a trifle with ladyfingers and cherry jam, and decorated it with mint leaves and cranberries that looked like a holly sprig. I made scalloped potatoes and green bean casserole and sausage stuffing, and wrapped them all up and stacked them in the refrigerator in the order they were supposed to go in the oven. I'm telling you, the invasion of Normandy couldn't have been planned better.

I was up at dawn, polishing and fluffing and shining and buffing. I stuffed the turkey and got it in the oven. I set the table and lit the candles. I chilled the wine. And then I realized I'd forgotten to make the eggnog. Well, of *course* we had to have eggnog while we were sitting around the Christmas tree opening presents after my beautiful meal. That was the plan, and my plan was not to be tampered with. There was nothing to do but send Richard out to the convenience store at the last minute for eggnog. What he came back with tasted like glue, but I could fix it. I poured it in a punch bowl, folded in some whipped topping from a spray can and a splash or two of rum, and covered the whole thing with grated nutmeg. It looked like the real thing. Almost.

Richard's parents arrived at noon, dressed to the nines and looking like visiting royalty in our tiny apartment, and weighted down with so many shopping bags and wrapped presents that you'd think they were bringing Christmas to orphans in a third world country. She was wearing a fur coat and diamond earrings and her hair was so perfectly done she looked like she'd just come from the beauty parlor that morning. She kissed the air beside my cheek and said, "Cecilia, you look exhausted!" There was no point in reminding her that my name was Celia. It wasn't that she didn't know what my name was; she just didn't like it. "I hope you didn't go to too much trouble. We would much rather have eaten out."

I told her it was no trouble at all and wished I'd had time to put on more lipstick. Of course I *was* exhausted, overheated, rumpled, and worn down to my last nerve. With four people, fifteen candles, a huge Christmas tree and a roasting turkey the apartment felt like a packing crate left on a dock in July, and the cute little red velveteen jumper and jacket I'd decided to wear didn't seem like such a good idea any more.

Once all the packages were piled under the tree the last of the floor space in the living room was used up, so there was no option except to line everyone up on the sofa and pass drinks and sausage balls to them over the counter from the kitchen. Richard's mother made a face when she tasted the wine and didn't touch the sausage balls, but kept a running dialogue going about all the people from Richard's past that I didn't know. Richard's father chewed his pipe and grunted now and then, and I stayed in the kitchen, sweating like a pig and growing sick of the smell of turkey. Naturally, I figured the best way to cool down and calm down was to sneak a quick cup of eggnog. It was a lot better than I had expected. In fact, it was the best store-bought eggnog I'd ever had. By the time the turkey was ready to serve, my mother-in-law's veiled insults were rolling off me like water off a duck's back. Even my father-in-law's stale joke about the three wise men was hilarious to me. I guess I was a little tipsy, which I couldn't understand because I had hardly put any rum in the eggnog at all.

The turkey turned out beautifully, if I do say so. Golden brown and shiny on top, crispy moist stuffing spilling from the cavity, it was a flawless first attempt. The table was gorgeous, set with our wedding china and silver, with a candle nestled in a champagne glass filled with cranberries in front of each place setting and an entire row of white pillar candles on evergreen bows running down the center of the table. Of course those candles did give off a lot of heat, so I helped myself to more eggnog as I was serving up the sides.

Richard's mother settled in at the table and declared, "How lovely everything looks, dear. And I'm so glad you felt comfortable enough with us not to bring out your good crystal. After all, we're family."

I didn't have a complete set of crystal yet, which she might have known if she had bothered to check our wedding registry, and the glasses I did have had been used to serve the wine. So I just smiled and took another slug of eggnog.

Richard squeezed into the kitchen to help carry the turkey. He took one look at me and was horrified. "You're drunk!" he accused in a stage whisper.

"I am not. All I've had is eggnog and I only put half a cup of rum in it."

He stared at me. "Rum?" He snatched my glass away. "I put half a bottle of brandy in it!"

It's funny how you don't realize how drunk you are until somebody tells you. I really started feeling woozy then.

Somehow we got the side dishes to the table and the turkey situated in front of Richard's father, who was given the honor of carving it. He was one of those men who liked to make a big show of sharpening the knife and making the expert butcher cuts, just like a pro. He made his first cut and I heard the distinctive crackle of plastic. Rookie mistake. I had forgotten to remove the little plastic bag of neck and giblets from the turkey cavity.

The look on everyone's face—especially Richard's—when his father pulled out that crunchy, charred-up bag of turkey organs struck me as funny, and I started to giggle. Then there was a big debate as to whether the rest of the turkey was edible, or whether the plastic might have poisoned the meat. That was even funnier. I couldn't stop laughing. Of course the parents were outraged and Richard was humiliated, but the best was yet to come.

Richard's father, whom I started to like a little better after that day, insisted the rest of the turkey was fine and started carving it up. His mother refused to allow the meat to be served until she inspected it. She leaned over to examine the platter, and when she did her perfectly styled hair brushed against the candle flame. It must have been loaded with hairspray, because it caught immediately—just a little flare, but it could have been a disaster. I threw the contents of my wine glass at her hair and before I could even register the look on her face—which, in retrospect, was worth everything—Richard jumped up and started beating out the smoke with his hands. I took the biggest breath I could manage and frantically blew out every candle on the table. Wax went everywhere—on the potatoes, the dinner rolls, into the green bean casserole, all over the turkey. When it was all over there was nothing left but the look of horror on my mother-in-law's face, and the smell of burned hair and hot wax in the air.

But the best was yet to come.

I felt just awful. The impression I had worked so hard to make was ruined. My mother-in-law had almost gone up in flames, every morsel of edible food was now covered in candle wax, my husband thought I was an idiot, and my head was throb-bing. I started to cry. And then the most remark-able thing happened.

My mother-in-law came around the table and hugged me. It was a real hug, too, not one of those fake Hollywood hugs I was used to from her. She patted my back and told me not to fret, Christmas dinner was overrated anyway, and besides, there was plenty of dessert and that was the best part of Christmas. Then she told me about her first holiday dinner, a Spam casserole in which she had managed to burn the Spam, and I began to think there might actually come a day—maybe sooner than I'd ever thought—when we would be friends.

That was when I threw up all over her silk blouse.

It wasn't all bad news, though. Two weeks later I found out I was expecting Lori. My mother-in-law and I did eventually become friends, too, but not until Richard and I were divorced. They would come out for the holidays every year while Lori was young, and every year she would tell Lori the story about the best Christmas ever: the Christmas we first knew that Lori was on the way.

Chapter Seven

In Which Mother's Intuition Rules

They were still chuckling when Lori's car door slammed and she bounded up the front steps, followed at a more sedate pace by Ida Mae.

"Hello, gorgeous," Paul greeted her, saluting her with a fruitcake cookie from the platter. "Your mom was just telling us about your first Christmas—the one before you were born."

Lori bent to kiss his cheek. "That's a good

story," she said. "But not as good as the one about Whiskers."

"Get over Whiskers, already," her mother said. "How was your drive?"

"It was great." She hugged Derrick and helped herself to a cookie. "How do you like the cookies?"

"The best I ever had," Derrick declared, and Lori cast a triumphant look at Ida Mae as she came up the steps.

"I told you," she said.

Ida Mae gave a little harrumph. "Better than nothing, I guess."

Lindsay said, "You didn't happen to pass Noah on the road, did you?"

Lori shook her head, munching the cookie. "Maybe he decided to go to Charlottesville, after all."

Lindsay's eyes widened with a mixture of alarm and disbelief. "He wouldn't do that. Not without telling me, he wouldn't. Not if he values his skin. Would he?"

Ida Mae pulled open the screen door and stopped short at the threshold. "What's that smell?" She turned a dark, suspicious look on the group on the porch. "Y'all didn't burn up my yeast rolls, did you? It takes four hours to make a good batch of rolls!"

"The rolls are fine," Bridget assured her quickly.

"It's a long story," Cici added.

Lindsay frowned a little into her empty glass. "I think I'll go call Noah. Just in case he does have some crazy idea about taking off for Charlottesville."

She got up and went inside, and Bridget, sighing wistfully over her own glass, rose as well. "As much as I'd like to sit here sipping and talking, I've got cookies to decorate."

"And I've got presents to wrap," Lori said.

Derrick stood too. "I'll get started on the pâté for tonight."

Cici said, "I guess that string of lights isn't going to fix itself."

Paul grinned at her. "Are you sober enough to get on a ladder?"

Lindsay came back to the door, looking worried. "Noah doesn't answer his phone."

"He's probably on his way home," Lori said, giving her a light pat on the shoulder as she passed. "You know he can't hear it over the noise of that motorcycle."

"He's supposed to keep it on vibrate. I told him to."

"You don't want him to answer the phone while he's driving," Bridget pointed out.

"I suppose not," Lindsay admitted, but she still looked troubled. "I wish he'd taken one of the cars."

Cici said, "Take the advice of someone who's been at this for awhile. If you worry about him like this every time he leaves the house, you won't survive the first year of motherhood, much less the rest of his life."

"I guess."

"It's the law of averages, sweetie," Paul said easily, getting to his feet. "How many times has he left the house on that motorcycle? And how many times has he come home safe and sound?"

Lindsay tried to look reassured, but didn't do a very good job. "I suppose."

Lori came back to the door. "Hey," she said, "what happened to the Christmas tree on the balcony?"

Cici grinned. "Aunt Lindsay will explain. And then the two of you can decide what to do about the empty space it left. Come on, Paul, help me get the ladder."

Perfume. In the end, all he had been able to find was perfume. He had looked at jewelry, but the gap between the dollars on the price tag and the dollars in his wallet was a little wide. Some salesgirl had tried to talk him into a sweater with pearl beads on it; easy for her to say in a store where the air conditioning was turned down to sixty. Coats, gloves, boots, scarves . . . the merchants had been no more prepared for a Christmas heat wave than the customers were.

Everybody else had been pretty easy. Bridget

had been after him for months to make her a knife rack, so he'd cut one out of red oak, tole-painted some Dutch flowers on it to match the tiles in the kitchen, and sealed it with his own compound of shellac and turpentine that gave it a nice soft shine and would stand up for years against kitchen grease and knife marks. For Cici, he'd painted a portrait of Lori sitting under a shade tree. Lori liked books with pictures of vampires on the covers, so he picked her up a couple from the drugstore. He got Ida Mae an apron with pot holders velcroed onto the pockets, because he thought that was cool. But Lindsay was different. She deserved something special.

The perfume was nice enough. It smelled like lilies, and it came in a gold box with blue velvet inside. But it was still perfume.

It was a good day for a ride once he got off the main highway and onto the more sparsely traveled mountain back roads. The air billowed his tee shirt and the sun baked his shoulders, and for a long stretch of road there was nothing but the pulse of the engine and the blue and lavender mountains curving behind the spiky branches of winter woodlands. He relaxed and eased back on the throttle, enjoying the scenery and trying not to worry about the stupid perfume. After all, Lori thought it was good enough for her mom. And she had been giving Christmas presents a lot longer than he had.

Except for a few tall pines and scrawny cedars, the trees on either side of the road looked naked and exposed: A squirrel's nest here, a few dead leaves clinging there. But then he saw something that made him look twice. Nestled in the fork of a tree a few hundred feet back into the woods was a cluster of green mistletoe. One of the few good memories he had of his dad was going out at Christmastime and tramping through the crisp cold woods, shooting down mistletoe with a twenty-two. His dad would cut it up and sell it to tourists and Christmas tree lots and such. Of course that had been before he turned completely drunk and the law took his guns . . . or maybe he sold them for more rye whiskey, Noah had never known. But those days hunting for mistletoe had been nice.

He came around a curve and spotted a dirt road going off into the woods that looked as though it might lead right up next to the tree with the mistletoe. On impulse, he turned hard left onto the road. He didn't see the white van barreling toward him until it was too late. He swerved right, the van swerved left. His front tire caught a patch of gravel and went into a skid. The motorcycle flew out from under him, and that was the last thing he knew.

"I think," Lori decided, surveying the empty balcony from below, "a Nativity scene. A big one, with sheep made out of cotton balls."

"Very funny." Lindsay regarded the empty space with folded arms, affecting thoughtfulness, but her expression was distracted.

"Whoever heard of two Christmas trees, anyhow?" Ida Mae observed disdainfully, moving past them with a broom to sweep the porch. "Miss Emily never saw the need for more than one tree. It's a blessing you didn't set the house afire with the dang fool thing."

"I'll agree with that, Ida Mae," Lindsay said. "It's a blessing." Her eyes wandered toward the telephone. "Maybe I'll try Noah again."

"You just called him five minutes ago," Lori said with a touch of exasperation. "You keep that up and he'll never come home. How about a big wreath?"

Lindsay replied absently, "We've got too many wreaths already."

"It can be a theme."

"You got bigger problems than what kind of worthless Christmas decorations to crowd up the landing with," Ida Mae said. "Fifty people coming tomorrow and the house smells like burnt shoes. What're you gonna do about that?"

All the windows were open, the fans were on, and the air-exchange system that cooled the house in the summer was going full blast in an effort to rid the house of the odor. A happy side effect was, of course, that the house was pleasantly cool for the first time in days.

"We'll boil some cinnamon sticks and orange peels on the stove," Lindsay replied. "It'll be fine."

Ida Mae gave another harrumph, and went out to sweep the porch.

"Poinsettias?" suggested Lori.

Lindsay glanced uneasily toward the phone again and rubbed her bare arms, as though chilled. "Did you ever get a bad feeling about something?"

Lori, who could be very single-minded, looked at her in bewilderment. "Not about poinsettias."

Lindsay gave a small laugh, and seemed to forcefully shake off her preoccupation. "Come on," she said, "help me get some buckets from the barn. I have an idea."

They took five gallon feed buckets, spray painted them gold, and banded each one with a red velvet ribbon. Then they lined them up behind the railing of the balcony and filled them with towering evergreen clippings from the cedar trees that grew along the fence line of the sheep pasture. Lindsay decorated the branches with glittering red glass balls carefully selected from the big Christmas tree in the parlor.

"Terrific," declared Bridget from the foyer below. "You know, I think I like that better than having a Christmas tree up there. And you can't even see the smoke smudges on the wall."

"I don't know," Lori said, standing beside her. "I think it needs lights."

"No lights!" chorused Bridget, Lindsay, Derrick and Cici, who came through the front door just then, followed by Paul.

Cici added, "The string on the outside of the house is up again. We tested it, and all systems go."

"I like the monochromatic theme," Paul said, admiring Lindsay's work.

"I hope the chickens won't mind being fed out of gold buckets," Bridget said, a little uncertainly.

"It'll make them feel like rock stars," Cici assured her.

"It's too bad all the ornaments were broken when the tree fell," Lori said. "I still think it needs a little something."

Cici said suddenly, "Maybe you're right. More red ornaments would be perfect."

Paul said, "I don't know. I like it like that. Minimalist."

"Minimalist is not exactly the Ladybug Farm style," Cici pointed out.

Lindsay said, "Listen to the expert, Cici. The man writes a style column for over sixty syndicated newspapers. It's fine. And I'm over this. Is there any more eggnog?"

Cici turned to Paul, her eyes wide with

unspoken meaning. "Paul, you don't mind running into town and trying to find another box of red ornaments, do you?"

Paul locked his gaze onto hers, clearly trying to read the subtext while he said hesitantly, "I guess not."

"The general store is open until five today," Cici said, taking his arm and turning him toward the door.

Lindsay straightened up and peered over the balcony, her face creased with alarm. "Is it that late?"

Cici walked Paul to the door. "Listen," she said, sotto voce, "I don't want to add to Lindsay's hysteria, but it's not like Noah to blow off chores when he knows how important this is to us. Maybe you could just drive to town and see if you see him anywhere?"

Paul's eyes darkened with concern. "You're not really worried are you?"

She shrugged a little, but her brow was knotted thoughtfully. "There is such a thing as mother's intuition, you know."

"I'm not one to argue with that. On my way." And then he smiled. "I'll even try to find you a box of red Christmas ornaments."

He started toward the door. Cici caught his arm, casting a quick, furtive glance back toward Lindsay. "Maybe," she added softly, moving close to him, "when you get to town and get cell phone reception, you could call the state patrol and see if there've been any accidents."

Paul met her eyes for a moment, and then nodded soberly. Then he turned and gave a cavalier wave toward the balcony. "More glass ornaments," he called, "definitely. Be back before you know it."

Lindsay's brows drew together unhappily. "That's what Noah said six hours ago."

The screen door closed behind him and Lori said, "We've got plenty of ornaments on the big tree. Maybe we could just steal some more. Oh! I know!" She hurried toward the parlor. "We can take my old Raggedy Ann doll, and that antique train car, and the teddy bear, and make a vignette . . ."

"No," Lindsay said firmly. She started down the stairs. "Not the teddy bear. He stays on the tree."

Derrick said, casting a critical eye toward the balcony, "I don't know what Paul is thinking. It doesn't need a thing."

"Maybe a few sprigs of holly," suggested Bridget.

Lindsay stood beside him and gazed up at the arrangement critically. "A little mistletoe wouldn't hurt."

Cici glanced at her. "What is the deal with that teddy bear, anyway? You've had it on your Christmas tree every year since I've known you."

Lindsay glanced at her, looked a little embarrassed, and made a wry face. "Longer than that, actually."

Bridget said, "Come to think of it, I've noticed that too. What's the story?"

Derrick said, "It sounds to me like it's time for a break."

"It sounds to me like it's time for more eggnog," Lindsay said. "It's low-cal, right?"

Derrick grinned and lifted a warning finger as he left the room. "Don't start till I get back."

Lindsay looked at Cici, trying to keep her expression, and her tone, calm. "Noah knows we're having dinner in a few hours. He wouldn't do this on purpose."

Cici slipped her arm through Lindsay's and turned her toward the parlor. "Come on, let's sit in here by the tree where it's cool, and take a break. We've been working all day. What's the point of Christmas if you can't enjoy it?"

Lori said curiously, "Seriously, Aunt Lindsay. What's the story with the teddy bear?"

Lindsay hesitated, and then her lips twisted into a reluctant smile. "Well it's kind of silly, really. Just something that happened to me when I was a little girl . . ."

Chapter Eight
Ghosts of Christmas Past: Lindsay

My mother and daddy divorced when I was seven and my sister was nine, and that was not an easy year for me. We moved out of our house into a little duplex apartment that didn't even have a back yard. I had to go to a new school, and I didn't have any friends. The only way I could cope with it all was by convincing myself that my daddy was coming back any minute now to make everything all right again. My sister was brutal about trying to disabuse me of my fantasy; being the oldest, she was probably the most hurt, and she felt it was her duty to make sure everyone else around her hurt as much as she did. Looking back, I know that my sister had an even worse time of it than I did, but all I could see then was that she was always picking on me.

My mother got a job at a department store and the two of us had to go to a babysitter after school. All I remember about our babysitter was that she was a dour old woman who gave me butter on saltines for a snack and made me sit at the dinette set and look at picture books while she watched her soap operas on television. Suze was okay; she had homework to do. But there were only two picture books for me, and after the first couple of days I had them memorized. My mother was always so tired when she picked us up, and we ate a lot of boxed macaroni and cheese for dinner.

As the holidays approached, my mother had to work longer hours. She was in retail, after all, but I think she was also trying to put aside a little extra for our Christmas. The problem was that the babysitter wouldn't keep us after six. So my mother would come and pick us up on her dinner break, and take us back to work with her. This was back in the day before malls, and the department store in town was the big-deal go-to place for Christmas shopping. But it was also a place where everybody knew everybody else, and as long as we were well-behaved and didn't get in the way we were welcome to hang out in the break room while our mother worked the last three hours of her shift.

For me it was a paradise. Can you imagine? A seven year old set down smack dab in the middle of Toyland? But of course my big sister had to be all bossy and in-your-face know-it-all. She figured that since Dad left it was her job to be in charge. Too bad she was the only one who saw it that way.

The store had an on-site Santa set up in the middle of the toy department, surrounded by a fake winter wonderland of plastic evergreens and cotton batting, with a peppermint striped North Pole marker and plaster reindeer suspended overhead on wires. My sister couldn't wait to tell me that Santa Claus was a fake. Well, I knew that. Everyone knew that the department store Santas just worked for the *real* Santa Claus, because he was too busy at Christmas to be everywhere at once. Besides, the Santa Claus display was, for me, the least impressive part of the store. What I was enchanted with, what I coveted and adored, was the Christmas tree that stood in the entrance of the store. It was covered with white lights, and every branch was decorated with a white teddy bear with a red plaid ribbon around its neck. The teddy bears were the department store's mascot—Tedmore was the name of the owner—and every teddy bear represented a needy child that the store customers were sponsoring for Christmas. Of course, I didn't know that. All I saw was a Christmas tree filled with teddy bears, and I was sure some lucky kid was going to get them all for Christmas.

My mother was determined to make this first Christmas without our dad as normal as it could be, and she did her best. There was a guy selling Christmas trees out in front of the store and she managed to talk him into a half-off discount for a scraggly little pine that was half dead when we got it, and she kept us busy making paper chains and popcorn strings to dress it up. I thought it was fun until my sister started calling it the "poor people's tree" and told me the only presents we'd be getting that year would be poor people's presents, because the only Santa Claus there had ever been was our daddy dressed up in a Santa suit, and since we didn't have a daddy any more Christmas wouldn't be coming this year.

Well of course I knew better than to believe anything Suze said. I knew there was a Santa Claus, just like I knew my daddy was coming back. But now I knew when: Christmas Eve.

Of course, I was worried about the Christmas tree, and I thought Suze might be right about that. Maybe Santa would be embarrassed to leave our presents under the poor people's tree, and I didn't want my daddy to come home and see our scraggly little tree with all its needles falling off and only one string of lights. I'd already written my letter to Santa Claus—or at least my mother had written it for me—but the next night when we went to work with Mother I sneaked off to see the department store Santa. I told him to forget the doll and the two-wheeler I had asked for; all I really wanted for Christmas was the teddy bear tree.

I didn't tell another soul what I'd asked for. I wanted it to be a surprise for everyone on Christmas morning to see what Santa had brought, and I especially wanted to see the look on my big sister's smart-aleck face.

Somehow my mother managed to put a few little presents under the tree, but we could tell by shaking them that they were mostly clothes—

gloves and socks and scarves and underwear. But of course everyone knew all the good stuff came from Santa.

On Christmas Eve, the store closed at six, so Mother picked us up directly from the babysitter and we went right home. But when we got there our door was hanging on its hinges and everything inside was a mess. The Christmas tree was knocked over and all the presents were gone. So was our television set and my mother's jewelry box, and when my mother saw that the closet she always kept locked was empty, she just sat down on the floor and started crying.

The police came, and I remember thinking the red lights that were flashing against the window had something to do with Christmas. My sister ran away and locked herself in her room, but I clung to my mother's skirts while she gave the police an inventory of everything that had been stolen. And then I heard her listing things like a Barbie Dream House and a girl's bicycle and a baby doll—all the things that my sister and I had asked Santa for. My mother had taken the job at the department store for the employee discount, and she had been putting things aside all year so that her girls would have a good Christmas. She had finally paid off the last toy only that week, and had locked everything away in the storage closet. Then a thief had broken into our house and taken it all.

My sister had been right. There was no Santa Claus. And this year, there wouldn't even be a Christmas. I will never forget the look on my mother's face when she told Suze and me how sorry she was. She started to cry, and so did Suze. And I could tell neither one of them were crying about Santa Claus.

We all slept together in the same bed that night, because we were too afraid to sleep by ourselves. But when Suze and I woke up on a very cold and gray Christmas morning, our mother was not there. We hurried out of bed to find her, but not because of the usual Christmas-morning excite-ment. Our world no longer had any magic in it. It wasn't even safe. And we just wanted our mother.

But when we got to the living room, we stopped dead. The room was overflowing with magic. There was a bicycle and a Dream House and an EasyBake oven and a baby doll in a pink silk dress. There were wrapped presents and two fat stockings overflowing with candy. And in the middle of it all was a gorgeous Christmas tree decorated with white lights and dozens of white teddy bears with plaid ribbons around their necks. My mother stood in front of it with her hands pressed to her cheeks, smiling so broadly I thought her face would break.

Santa Claus had come after all, and if I live to be a hundred, I'll never have a better Christmas.

Chapter Nine

In Which Noah Sees an Angel

"That's the best Christmas story ever, Aunt Lindsay," Lori said. She sat on the floor beside the Christmas tree, her arms wrapped around her updrawn knees, her eyes bright with approval. "Well," she felt compelled to add, "one of the best anyway. It reminds me of Whiskers."

Cici ignored her deliberately. "So where did all the presents come from?" she asked Lindsay. "Did the police find your stuff?"

Lindsay shook her head, smiling as she removed the faintly tattered white teddy bear from the tree and straightened its plaid bow. "No, but the officers who came out felt so bad about a single mother with two kids losing all their gifts on Christmas Eve that they took up a collection and replaced as many things from the evidence list as they could. They even got Tedmore's to open up special for them, and when the manager heard that it was one of his employees . . ."

"He donated the teddy bear tree!" Bridget exclaimed, clapping her hands in delight. "And that's one of the bears, after all these years?"

Lindsay nodded and tucked the bear carefully back into place. "The best part was that, after that, my sister actually started to believe in Santa Claus again."

Derrick grinned and topped off her glass from the eggnog pitcher. "Now that's what I call a Christmas miracle. I've met your sister."

Lindsay sighed a little, gazing into her glass without tasting it. "I'm starting to think another Christmas miracle wouldn't be unwelcome right about now."

She put the glass on the coffee table and walked to the window, thrusting her hands into the pockets of her shorts as she looked out. The shadows of the mountains lay in deep purple stripes over the sheep meadow as the light began to leach out of the day. Rebel was busily circling and bunching his sheep toward the shelter at the south end of the meadow, a ritual he performed every dusk, whether anyone wanted him to or not. The chickens were quiet, having already gone in to roost. The goat rested on its folded knees atop the thatched roof of the goat house, and Bambi nibbled acorns from beneath the big oak tree in the front yard. The driveway curved like a silver Christmas ribbon toward the road, still and quiet.

And empty.

Noah saw a bright light and blurry white face surrounded by a golden halo. He said, "Am I dead?"

A female voice replied shortly, "Not unless I kill you. Wiggle your fingers."

He did as instructed, squeezed his eyes shut, and opened them again slowly. The figure became more distinct: a young woman with golden blond hair tumbled over her face, and eyes as blue as the December sky. He said, "Are you an angel?"

"Very funny, cowboy." She sounded mad, and she was poking at his arms and his ribs and legs. He struggled to sit up.

His head hurt like crazy and he was dizzy for a minute, but he heard her say, "I don't think anything is broken. You're a hell of a lot luckier than you deserve."

She sat back on her heels, scowling at him, and snatched up his blue helmet from the ground. It had a starburst crack in it. "You see this, hot-shot?" She pointed at the crack in the helmet, her eyes flashing. "That would have been your *head* if you hadn't been wearing this."

"Hey!" He grabbed the helmet from her. "My—" he started to say "mom" but changed it to, "Somebody gave me that!" He stared at the crack in the shiny blue surface, and felt a little woozy. He tossed the helmet back down on the ground in disgust, and struggled to his feet. The woman—who he now realized was no angel—watched him cautiously, as though she was getting ready to catch him if he fell down.

Every bone in his body felt as though it had

been through the tumble-dry cycle at the Laundromat, but his legs held firm. He looked around for his bike, and saw a glint of chrome poking up from a shallow gully a few dozen yards away. He moved toward it, limping a little, as fast as he was able, sliding a few feet down the pine straw–covered slope where the mangled corpse of his motorcycle lay. He stared at it in dismay for a moment. The front wheel was twisted almost perpendicular to the frame, the crankcase cover was missing, the back wheel was turned sideways, the headlight shattered. Oil dripped onto the carpet of dried leaves with a steady tick-tick sound. He plucked a leafy vine from the spokes of the front wheel, then tossed it to the ground, swearing loudly. It was dead, wrecked, completely useless. For good measure, he kicked the machine soundly in the handlebars, which did nothing but cause a sharp pain to shoot up his leg. He swore again.

"Real mature." The woman stood a few feet above him, her hands on her hips. "You got a phone?"

He walked around the broken motorcycle in disgust. "Use your own phone." He wrenched the saddlebags off the back of the bike, but a tell-tale aroma gave him the bad news even before he opened the buckle. The pretty gold box was crushed flat. Broken glass rattled, and lily-scented perfume soaked the leather. He pulled the box out and tossed it on the ground.

She said, "I don't have one."

"One what?"

"Phone."

Noah opened the strap on the other saddlebag. Inside was a tool kit, a couple of crushed candy bars, a sketch pad, the remnants of some shattered charcoal pencils, and his phone—now in three pieces. He picked the pieces up and dropped them, one by one, on the ground beside the gold box. The woman walked away.

Noah squatted on the ground and surveyed the ruins of his Christmas for a moment. Muscles he had never even known he had before throbbed like fire. Even his teeth hurt. And Lindsay was going to be as mad as a cat with its tail caught in a door. He should have been home hours ago. He still had chores to do. He'd promised to help with the windows, and if he wasn't there to do it, Cici would get up on that ladder by herself. Sometimes he didn't know how those women had managed at all before he came along. And now here he was, stranded in the middle of nowhere with no wheels, wasting time when there wasn't any time to waste. He picked up the pieces of the phone and tried to fit them together again. He even tore off a strip of electrical tape from the toolkit and tried to weld the casing and the battery back together again, but no dice.

Lindsay was going to kill him. No two ways about it.

He got up slowly and climbed back up to the dirt road. He looked around for the woman, but all he saw was a set of skid marks going off the road and down the embankment. He followed them and saw a white minivan in the woods about ten feet below the level of the road, resting catty-cornered on two wheels and leaning against a tree. The driver's side door was open and the blond-haired woman had one foot against the floorboard and her hands on the doorframe, trying to rock the van back onto its four wheels.

"Hey," Noah called.

She didn't stop. He watched her for a moment.

"You planning to drive it on up here when you get it straight?"

"You got a better idea?"

"You got four wheel drive?"

She paused and looked up at him, and when she did that blond hair of hers fell away from her face. He couldn't help staring.

Her left cheekbone was a twisted knot that made her eye look as though it had been sewn shut at the corner. Part of her eyebrow was gone, and at her jawbone there was an odd indentation, as though part of it was missing. The other side of her face was the face of an angel. This side was not.

She quickly ducked her head and went back to rocking the car. She put as much force into it as a grown man, and the springs creaked and groaned. The van swayed. Nothing happened.

Noah came down the hill. He opened the side door and grabbed the roofline, putting his shoulder against the frame. They worked in silence for four or five minutes, until sweat was rolling down Noah's sides and dripping from his nose, and he had to stop to swipe an arm across his face so that he could see.

"This is bull," he said, breathing hard. "We don't have enough room for leverage. Even if we get it straight it ain't going anywhere."

She sank back against a tree, bracing her hands on her knees, breathing hard. She was a skinny woman, wearing jeans and a baggy blue tee shirt, older than Lori but maybe not quite thirty. Her head was down so he couldn't see her face. "This isn't my car," she said. "I borrowed it from a friend. Some friend I turned out to be. Why the hell did you have to come flying around that corner like a crazy person? None of this would have happened if it wasn't for you!"

He felt bad about that. He wiped another stream of sweat from his forehead and was quiet for a minute. Then he said, "A tow chain can get it out. It doesn't look too messed up. Maybe your friend won't be too mad."

She lifted her head long enough to shoot him a dark look. "Do you happen to have a spare tow chain on you?"

Noah blew out a breath. He looked up at the sky through the fingers of the trees, and it seemed to him the color was getting paler. He didn't have a watch, but he didn't need one to know it was late. He muttered, "What kind of grown woman doesn't have a phone, anyhow?"

She answered, pushing away from the tree, "The kind that doesn't have any money."

She started to heave her weight against the car again, but Noah caught her shoulder. "Come on," he said. "Give it up."

She glared at him for a moment, then jerked away. She turned back to the van, then drew back and kicked the front tire with all her might.

Noah said, "Real mature."

She reached inside the car, grabbed her purse, and stalked up the hill. Noah stood beside the car for a minute, trying to think of something that would help. Finally, angry and frustrated with himself, he climbed back up the hill. She had already reached the paved road, and was walking in the direction from which he had come.

"Hey!" he called.

She just kept walking.

"Hey, where are you going?"

"Where do you think?" she tossed back over her shoulder. "To find civilization."

"Well, you won't find it that way."

Her steps slowed. After a moment, she turned and came back toward him. "What are you talking about?"

He shrugged. "There's nothing up that road but

cow pastures for twenty miles. I just came that way." He jerked his head over his shoulder in the direction from which her car had come. "What's back there?"

She scowled and hunched her shoulders as she trudged closer, her head ducked. "I don't know. I guess I got kind of lost. The next thing I knew I was on this dirt road. I guess I'd been driving it about half an hour. I didn't see any houses. The van doesn't have a GPS."

Noah looked around unhappily, screwing up his face as he measured the shadows on the road. "There's a county road about five miles south," he said, at last. "Maybe we can pick up a ride. The nearest town's at least half an hour away by car."

"Terrific," she muttered. She turned back toward the paved road. "Thanks a lot, kid. See you around."

"Hey."

She looked back impatiently.

"Didn't you say you were lost?"

"So?"

He shrugged. "So I've been living around here all my life. Spent most of it walking. You got a flashlight?"

She scowled. "What for?"

"It'll be getting dark pretty soon. Lots of critters around these woods at night. They mostly stay away from light, though."

She looked around uneasily, then back at him. Her expression said she wasn't sure whether he was pulling her leg or not. She straightened her shoulders and turned on her heel and started back to the road. Then she whirled back and demanded impatiently, "Well? Are you coming or not?"

He grinned. "Hold on a sec."

He went back into the woods a few dozen yards until he found the tree. He grasped the lower branch and, sore muscles protesting, hoisted himself up. She stood on the road, watching in disbelief.

"What are you? Crazy?"

"After all this, I'm not going home without what I came here for. I'm going to be in enough trouble as it is."

He found foothold and handhold and pulled himself up through the branches until he found the cluster of mistletoe. He used his pocketknife to cut it loose, and watched as it fell to the leafy ground below. He climbed down more rapidly than he had ascended, dropped lightly to the ground, and picked up the mistletoe.

The woman was watching him, agape. "Mistletoe?" she said, incredulously. "You wrecked my car and your bike, could've gotten yourself killed—not to mention me—and stranded us both in the middle of the woods for *mistletoe?*"

He picked up his saddlebags, tucked the

mistletoe carefully inside, and swung the bags over his shoulder. "It's Christmas," was all he said. "You about ready?"

Wordlessly, she fell into step beside him.

Chapter Ten

In Which It's Always Darkest Before the Dawn

Ida Mae said, "About what time are y'all figuring on eating supper?"

"When everybody gets here, that's when," Lindsay snapped at her, and Ida Mae drew back, puffing out her chest.

"You don't need to bite my head off. I've got a bread pudding, to bake, you know. And that turkey's already been resting half an hour. You want me to start carving or not?"

"Oh, no, don't carve yet," Bridget said, moving toward the kitchen. "I haven't even started the cranberries."

"And I need to get the asparagus puffs in the oven," Derrick said.

Ida Mae looked at him skeptically. "What in blazes are asparagus puffs?"

"Little bites of heaven, my darling," he assured her, slipping his arm through hers. "Little bites of heaven."

"Whoever heard of asparagus this time of year?" She still sounded disgruntled, although not even she was immune to Derrick's notorious charm.

"Californians."

Cici got to her feet as the three of them disappeared toward the kitchen. "I guess I'll go feed the animals."

Lindsay said sharply, "That's Noah's job."

"Well, Noah's not here," Cici replied patiently, "so unless you want the goat and the deer and the dog to go without dinner on Christmas Eve . . ."

"Hey," Lori said suddenly, "someone's coming."

The three of them rushed to the front porch, and stood watching in disappointment as Paul pulled up. He got out of the car but the truth was on his face even before he met Cici's eyes and said, "Sorry. No red Christmas ornaments."

Lindsay turned toward the house. "I'm calling the police."

Paul gave Cici an apologetic look as he started up the steps. "Actually, I stopped by the police station on my way back."

Lindsay turned expectantly.

"They were very nice. They even checked with the hospital and the state patrol. No motorcycle accidents," he assured them quickly. "But they said they'd keep an eye out. Of course," he added reluctantly, "they're running a skeleton crew."

Lindsay said, "I'll get my car keys. We need to start checking the roads."

"I'll help," Lori volunteered quickly.

Cici threw up a hand. "Stop, both of you. Nobody's going to do any such thing."

"I checked the roads between here and town," Paul said. "I even went down some of the back roads. Almost hit a deer on one, and got chased by a pit bull on another."

"It's going to be dark in half an hour," Cici said, "and you can't check every road in this part of the state. What if he did go to Charlottesville, and got caught in mall traffic? How's it going to help to have you two wandering around out there lost while Noah's here waiting to have his Christmas dinner? Just calm down." She pushed a hand through her hair and added deliberately, clearly speaking more to herself than to them, "Everyone . . . just calm down."

Cici drew and released a deep breath. "Lori, go get Bambi's corn. I'll get the goat chow and feed the dog."

Paul put his arm around Lindsay's shoulders. "Come on, hon," he said, "let's set the table. I'll bet he'll be back before we're done."

Lindsay bit her lip. "What if he's not?"

"Then," replied Paul simply, "we'll wait."

They had gone about a mile before Noah said, "What's your name?"

She didn't look at him. "Kathy."

"Mine's Noah."

She said nothing.

"Where're you from?"

"Philly."

"Oh, yeah? Pennsylvania?"

"You got it, genius."

"You got family here or something?"

"No."

"Then what're you doing wandering around in the mountains getting lost on Christmas Eve?"

"Why do you have to ask so many questions?"

"I don't. Don't care who you are, where you're from, what kind of trouble you're in. I'm just walking."

She slid a dark glance toward him. "I'm not in trouble."

He said nothing. They walked another couple of hundred feet in silence.

She said, "That's a pretty fancy-smelling saddle-bag."

He frowned. "Perfume busted. It was a present."

"For your girlfriend?"

"Nah. For my mom." That felt funny to say. "Not really my mom. Just kind of."

"How can somebody be kind of your mom?"

He frowned deeper. "Just is, that's all."

He stopped suddenly, cocking his head. "Listen." Then he grabbed her arm and pulled her to the side of the road. "Car's coming!"

They turned to greet the sedan that appeared around the corner, waving excitedly. The driver, a woman with a dress bag hanging in the back and a passenger seat filled with packages, returned a cheery "Merry Christmas!" wave and zoomed past, leaving nothing but a whoosh of hot air in her wake.

Kathy shouted after her, "Thanks a lot, lady!" She stepped back on the asphalt angrily and started walking again. "So much for the Christmas spirit."

"Hey come on," Noah said. "She didn't know us. She probably didn't even know we needed a ride."

"Oh yeah, lots of people go walking at dusk on a deserted road carrying their purse and a set of motorcycle saddlebags. How much further to this county road of yours?"

"We'll see it when we get there."

The dusk grew deeper, and the air a little cooler. The only sound was the crunch of their footsteps on the shoulder and the occasional scurry of a squirrel or a rabbit in the woods beyond.

After a time he said, "So what happened to your face?"

He didn't expect her to answer, and was surprised when she did.

"Iraq happened," she said briefly.

"Hey, no kidding?" His footsteps slowed and he looked at her. "You were a soldier?"

"I was a medic."

"That," he declared, "is cool."

"It wasn't cool," she said roughly. "It was a war. There's nothing cool about it. I got to spend eighteen months putting pieces of soldiers back together and two days before I was supposed to deploy stateside to be with my fiancé an IED took out my jeep and my driver, and I spent the next eight months in a hospital while doctors tried to put *me* back together, and there's nothing cool about that, kid, not one damn thing."

She walked faster. He let her. After awhile she got tired, and slowed back to a normal pace. He caught up with her not long after that.

"So where is he now? Your fiancé?"

"I don't know." She sounded tired when she said it, as though all her anger had worn her out. "We met over there, you know. He was in my unit. You get to know a person really fast and . . . well. He went home three months before me, and we planned to get married in his home town. Then a bomb changed everything."

"He broke up with you?"

She didn't look at him. "I knew he'd never break up with me, not if he knew what had happened. But I didn't want his pity, and how could I keep him tied to this?" She made a brief gesture toward her face. "Besides, there was a while there that they didn't even know how bad I was hurt. There was some nerve damage, and they didn't know if I'd ever get back the use of my left side again. It was going to be months of rehab, and I still might never recover. He hadn't signed up to be nursemaid to a cripple for the rest of his life. He deserved better. So I e-mailed him from the hospital, and told him I'd decided to re-up. That I'd realized what we had was just a war fling, and now that he was gone I'd lost interest. I broke up with him." She trudged along with her head down, her hands gripping the strap of her purse that was slung across her chest. "He wouldn't accept it at first, sent a lot of e-mails, wrote letters . . . but I never read them. Never answered."

Noah walked beside her in silence while the last of the light left the sky. He said after awhile, "I think he deserved to know, and make up his own mind."

He heard a soft sound, like a sigh. "Yeah. I think so too. I had a lot of time to think in the hospital. I even sent him an e-mail, but it bounced back. He'd closed the account. So my friend talked me into borrowing her van and driving to Charlottesville, where he lived, because something like this needs to be done in person anyway. Only he didn't live there anymore and his phone was disconnected and I didn't know how to find him, and it was Christmas Eve so I just started driving, and that's how I ended up here, lost." She hesitated, and he thought she glanced at him. "I guess maybe it wasn't all your fault, the accident.

Maybe I wasn't paying as much attention as I should have been."

He'd figured as much. He just hadn't wanted to say it.

"So what are you going to do?" he asked.

"Nothing. I don't know. What can I do? I've got to get a job, find a place to live, do something with my life. It was stupid, trying to find him. I should've left well enough alone. I thought I could change everything just because I changed my mind and . . . it was stupid."

Noah stopped suddenly at a place where the weeds and grasses of the shoulder flattened out into a narrow dirt road. "I know this road." He was cautiously excited. "It ends up right in front of our sheep pasture. It's only about an hour's walk."

She looked at him skeptically. "It's not a road, it's a cow path. It doesn't look to me like it ends up anywhere."

"I'm telling you, this was my shortcut to town before I got wheels. I know where I'm going."

"It's getting dark. We should stay on the main roads."

He shrugged. "Suit yourself. But I'm hungry, and we're having turkey and gravy with mashed potatoes for supper, and Ida Mae's bread pudding." He reached into his saddlebags, found the steel-cased flashlight, and switched it on. A pleasant yellow cone of light dispersed the

112

shadows on the dirt road, and he followed it. "If you turn south on the county road," he said, "after about four or five hours, you'll come to a sign at the end of a driveway that says 'Ladybug Farm.' I'll tell them to save you some turkey in case you get hungry before you get to town."

She let him go about ten feet down the road, and then, swearing under her breath, she followed him.

The dining room table was set with a crisp white cloth, glittering crystal and china, and a votive candle wrapped in holly at each place setting. The napkin rings were silver ribbons tied with gold ornaments, and the centerpiece was a low table-cape of evergreen, white candles, and gold glass balls. Paul took out his cell phone and snapped a picture. It was stunning. All that remained to be done was the pouring of the wine, the lighting of the candles, and, of course, the gathering of the family.

The aromas of sweet potato casserole, baking rolls and sausage gravy drifted out onto the front porch where everyone had wandered, one by one, to watch the sunset. That had been over an hour ago. A low cloud cover had begun to move in over a purple sky, obscuring even the stars, and the driveway, which they all watched so fixedly, remained black and empty. The screen door squeaked open and closed and all heads swiveled toward Lindsay as she came outside.

But she was shaking her head. "I talked to the local police and the state patrol," she said, "and the hospitals between here and Charlottesville. Nothing. The police said if we don't hear from him in a couple of hours they'll send a man out to take a report, like that would do any good."

She walked to the front of the porch and rested her hand on the column, looking out over the black lawn. "It sure is dark."

"It's clouding up," said Bridget. "Maybe we'll get some rain to break the humidity."

Lindsay said, "I don't think Noah took his rain suit."

"We should turn the Christmas lights on," Lori said suddenly. "It's Christmas Eve after all."

"You're right, Lori," Cici said, forcing enthusiasm. "I love sitting on the porch under the glow of the Christmas lights, and how many Christmas Eves is it warm enough to do that?"

"I'll turn on the Christmas tree," Bridget said.

"I'll get the window lights," Paul said.

"And I," declared Derrick, "will get the asparagus puffs and the bottle of Montrachet that I was positively assured will make any Christmas brighter."

When they were gone, Cici came up to Lindsay and put an arm around her shoulders. "You know what I've always admired about Noah?" she said. "He doesn't know the meaning of the word 'quit'."

Lindsay managed a smile. "He's pretty resourceful," she admitted.

"Remember when he saved up his whole summer's wages to buy that motorcycle?"

"He wasn't even old enough to drive."

"Didn't stop him."

"That thing's a death trap."

"Hardly. He keeps it in better shape than most people keep their cars."

"He spent most of his life living in campgrounds," Lindsay remembered. "Feeding and sheltering himself. How do you even *do* that?"

"And with more time spent out of the classroom than in it, he still managed to get a scholarship to one of the most prestigious private schools in the area."

Lindsay's face softened with pride. "He's really something."

"You know," said Cici, "I'm having a hard time thinking of any situation Noah couldn't handle."

Inside the house, the Christmas tree sprang to life, its multicolored lights spilling across the lawn from the front window. In another moment the wreaths in the upstairs windows sparkled with white lights, and then the downstairs window wreaths spread their glow across the night, illuminating the smile on Lindsay's face as she turned to Cici.

"You know something," she said, "you're right.

And you're also pretty good to have around in a crisis."

"Or any other time," Cici pointed out lightly, and Lindsay grinned.

"Right," she said, hugging her.

Paul held open the screen door for Derrick, who carried a tray of hors d'oeuvres and glasses. Lori followed with a bottle of wine and a corkscrew. "Louis Jadot Poligny '07," she said with admiration in her voice. "I've read about this. One of the best chardonnays to come out of Burgundy in a decade." Lori was studying enology in preparation for one day managing the Ladybug Farms vineyard and winery.

Cici said, "We're honored."

And Lindsay added, "You shouldn't have."

"Nonsense. What better occasion to open a fine bottle of wine than Christmas with friends?"

He set the tray on the wicker table, and Bridget came out onto the porch. "Oh wait," she said, "before you pour the wine, let's turn the outside lights on."

"I'll get it." Cici found the extension cord behind one of the rocking chairs while Derrick filled the glasses, and she plugged it in.

Paul stepped out into the yard to snap a picture. A chorus of "oohs" and "ahhs" went up as the icicle lights that were draped from the roofline of the porch came on all around the house, the gazebo in the side garden sprang to fairyland life with hundreds of miniature white lights, and the evergreens that flanked the walkway in front of the house were spiraled with lights. It was like a winter wonderland for forty-five full seconds.

And then the entire house was plunged into darkness.

Kathy said, "Are you sure you know where you're going?" Her breath sounded labored, and her tone short. "This is the right road, right?"

In fact, Noah wasn't nearly as sure as he should have been. It had been years since he'd taken this shortcut, and it was a lot more overgrown and rutted than he remembered. Moreover, his recollection was that it had run parallel to the country road in places, and they should have been seeing lights by now. The world around them was, instead, as black and silent as a tomb.

He said, "Yeah, sure." He cast the flashlight beam from side to side and saw nothing but brush and brambles. The beam was noticeably weaker, but he found no reason to point that out to his companion. "We're good."

"Because we've been walking a lot longer than an hour."

"Nah. Just seems that way." It seemed, in fact, more like two or three.

She said, "Hold on." Her voice sounded tight. "I've got to rest."

She took a few more steps and sank to the

ground, her left leg drawn up. When Noah swept the flashlight beam in her direction he could see her face was tight with pain as she kneaded her calf muscle. "Damn thing," she muttered, "still seizes up on me."

Noah switched the flashlight off to save the battery, and he squatted down in the dead grass across from her. He waited until his eyes adjusted to the dark and he could make out her shape in the starlight. Then he said, "My mom left me when I was a baby. She thought she was doing the right thing, left me with my grandma while she tried to get work. But then my grandma died, and I went to live with my dad, and my mom got on drugs and didn't know about any of it. When she got clean and tried to find me all those years later, I was gone."

He found a twig in the grass and started gouging the dirt with it in a desultory fashion. He could feel her eyes on him, and her fingers worked the muscles of her leg a little more slowly.

He said, "My dad was a mess, couldn't take care of his own self, much less a kid, so I was pretty much on my own. I kind of bounced from pillar to post, and then I heard about these three crazy women that had bought this big old house and thought they could fix it up by themselves. They looked like they had money, so I went to work for them, but they didn't pay much more than a fair wage. At least not in money. But when my dad died, they gave me a place to live, and an education, and a feeling that I belonged someplace, and they even found my mom for me. Turns out she'd been looking for me for years, but when my dad moved out of state, she lost track. Didn't know where to start."

He glanced at her, and she had stopped rubbing her leg. He could see her profile in the darkness, intent upon his face.

"But here's the thing," he said, "I was so mad at her for leaving, and so grateful to my new family for what they'd done—and maybe not wanting them to be mad at me—that I wouldn't see her, or talk to her, no matter how many times she called. After awhile, though, living with those women, seeing how they all were like a family even though they weren't related, and how they made me feel like I belonged there, even though I wasn't related . . . well, I started to feel a little more kindly to my mom. I wanted to see her. I tried to set something up with her. But by that time, she was dead."

That was still hard to say. He felt the words echo in the night. He saw them reflected in her shadow. He said, very quietly, "I guess I'll always wonder what I missed out on."

The night was eerily quiet. No crickets, no birds, no woodland creatures. She said, after a very long time, "I guess these days anybody can find anybody."

"It's not that hard. You hear about it all the time. Sometimes they use military records and stuff. I guess the person looking just has to want it bad enough."

She glanced at him, and then away. Her voice sounded muffled when she spoke. "What if he doesn't want me?"

"Then," Noah said, "I guess you won't have to wonder what you missed out on, will you?"

They listened to the silence for another short time. Then she said, "How old are you?"

"Seventeen."

She pushed herself to her feet. He could hear the groan that was suppressed under her breath. And she said, "You're pretty damn smart, you know that?"

He gave a half grin that he knew she couldn't see, and he stood as well. "Yeah. People tell me that. You ready?"

"Let's go."

He switched on the flashlight, and nothing happened.

The battery was dead.

One by one, Ida Mae lit each of the candles in the windows and covered them with glass hurricane shades. She came out onto the porch, holding her kerosene lantern high. "Y'all gonna change for supper, or come to the table looking like heathens?"

Paul glanced down at his bare legs and sandal-clad feet. "I wouldn't exactly say I look like a heathen," he offered defensively. "These sandals are by Salvatore Ferragamo."

Bridget came out behind Ida Mae. "You won't believe this. The power company says half the grid is down. It seems that with the heat wave everybody had their air conditioning going, and then plugging in their Christmas lights on top of it . . ."

"Wow," Lori said, a little in awe. "I knew about the curse of Ladybug Farm, but to blow out half the power grid . . ."

Cici scowled at her. "We did *not* blow out the power grid. It was a coincidence, that's all."

"Right," murmured Derrick, and quickly hid his expression in his wine glass.

"They're sending someone out," Bridget added, "but it might take awhile."

"Meantime, my gravy's getting cold and my turkey's going dry," Ida Mae said.

Bridget touched her arm lightly. "Maybe we could put the gravy back on the stove to keep it warm," she suggested, "and wrap up the turkey? It may be awhile before we eat."

Ida Mae ignored her. "What for? So you can sit out here feeling sorry for yourselves?" Her gaze was on Lindsay, who was leaning against the porch column with a glass of wine in her hand, gazing out at the empty night. "Seems to me like a dang fool thing to do on Christmas Eve."

Lindsay drew in a breath, and exhaled it a little unsteadily. "I'm not feeling sorry for myself," she said. "I'm feeling guilty. I've messed up everything. I was an idiot to think I could be a mother. I mean, he was half-grown when I adopted him, I guess I figured how hard could it be? All I really had to do was one thing: keep him safe. And I couldn't even do that."

Cici got up and embraced Lindsay with one arm. Bridget crossed the porch and slipped her own arm through Lindsay's, pressing her cheek briefly against her shoulder. Ida Mae said gruffly, "Seems to me that job is in hands a lot more powerful than yours, Missy, and if there was ever a night for having faith, this is it."

Lindsay turned slowly to look at her. Cici and Bridget gave her reassuring smiles. Paul and Derrick lifted their glasses to the three of them.

"She's right," Lori said. "It's just like Whiskers."

Ida Mae looked at her in exasperation. "Who the blazes is Whiskers?"

Lori smiled and settled into the rocking chair her mother had abandoned. "Well," she said.

Chapter Eleven

Ghosts of Christmas Past: Lori

When I was seven, I had this cat named Whiskers, a gray long-haired domestic with a white splotch on his nose. That cat was my best friend, he went everywhere with me. I'd dress him up in doll clothes and take him for a ride in my baby-doll buggy, and put him in the basket of my tricycle and cruise around the cul-de-sac, and have tea parties with him in the back yard, and read him stories from my picture books at night. And he was such a great cat, he actually let me do all those things and hardly ever complained. Well, he wasn't that crazy about wearing a bonnet, but other than that he was just as good as could be.

We were living in the house on Huntington Lane then—which is where Mom moved here from—and Aunt Bridget lived across the street with her kids, Kevin and Katie, and Aunt Lindsay lived next door to her. This was before Uncle Paul and Uncle Derrick moved to our neighborhood, but they had been friends with my mom and dad in Washington, and they would come visit for holidays and birthdays, and it was always a party when they came. Just like now. I mean, for my fifth birthday they rented an entire kiddie park with a bouncy house, pony rides *and* Cinderella's castle. And they always came for Christmas.

Mom and Dad were divorced, of course, and my dad had already moved to California. Mom had just opened her real estate office and she worked pretty long hours. Katie used to babysit me sometimes, and Aunt Lindsay was a teacher at my school. I was never in her class, although when Mom got stuck showing a house and couldn't pick me up after school I'd go sit in Aunt Lindsay's classroom and color while she graded papers, then I'd ride home with her. Usually we'd stop for ice cream, then go over to Aunt Bridget's for supper. Or sometimes we'd get pizzas and everyone would come over to my house to eat so that Mom wouldn't have to cook when she got home. Either way, Whiskers was always with me. Aunt Bridget wouldn't let him sit at the table—well, neither would Mom, to tell the truth—but other than that, he never left my side.

I hated taking the Christmas card photo—that much hasn't changed—but Mom told me that if Santa didn't get a Christmas card with a picture of everyone in the family he wouldn't know which house to bring the presents to. Naturally, I had to make sure Whiskers was in the photo. Mom and I had matching red velvet skirts and white lace blouses, and I had a big red velvet bow in my hair. I tied a matching red velvet bow with jingle bells on it around Whiskers' neck, but that wasn't good enough. I was determined to wrestle him into a Santa hat, too. We got all set up in front of the Christmas tree, but every time the photographer would fire the flash Whiskers would try to jump out of my lap, which knocked off his hat, which ruined the shot, and I'd spend another five minutes trying to get his hat on, and my mom was losing patience by the minute. So was the photographer, who charged by the hour and should have been happy, but was really just an old grouch. He told Mom there was an extra charge for working with animals, and she told *him* that if he didn't get his shot in the next two minutes he'd be lucky to get paid at all. So he started packing up his gear in a snit—which was great with me—and that was when my mom had her Big Idea. She decided to have two Christmas photos that year, one with Whiskers and one without. I wasn't about to agree, but she promised me a piece of the butterscotch-maple fudge she had made to give to my Sunday School teacher for Christmas, so I thought it might be okay if Whiskers wasn't in *every* picture, as long as he was in the main one. I sold out my own cat for a piece of butterscotch-maple fudge.

Well, the photographer got his picture, a beautiful one of me and mom in our velvet skirts and lace blouses, sitting in front of the Christmas tree and smiling at each other. Whiskers, without his Santa hat, just wandered around sniffing the photographer's equipment bag. But the minute that flash went off Whiskers jumped about a foot straight up in the air and knocked over one of the lights. The photographer tried to catch it and stepped on Whisker's tail. There was a lot of yowling and spitting, and when the photographer went outside to get another light, Whiskers flew right out the door.

I looked for him the rest of the day, door to door. He wasn't at Aunt Bridget's, or Aunt Lindsay's, or at the community pool or at any of the neighbor's houses. The next day Mom helped me make up posters with his picture on them, and we put them everywhere—on every tree and utility pole we could find, in every mail box, on the community bulletin board at the bank and the grocery store. I could tell Mom felt really bad about losing Whiskers, but the worst part was that he wasn't in the Christmas card photo. How would Santa know which house to bring our presents to?

What my mom couldn't bear to tell me was that the *real* worst part was that one of the neighbors had called and said he had seen a cat fitting our description on his way to work that morning—in a ditch on the side of the road, having been run over by a car. It was less than a week before Christmas. How could she tell me Whiskers was dead? I was already inconsolable. So she let me go on handing out flyers and walking up the street calling "Here, kitty, kitty" and running to the door each time the doorbell rang, expecting to see someone bringing Whiskers home. First thing every morning and the last thing at night, I'd rush to the back door and expect to see Whiskers there. I didn't want to play with my friends, I didn't want to go see Santa, I didn't want to help bake cookies. All I wanted was Whiskers. Mom decided there was only one solution: Whiskers had to come home.

She searched all over Baltimore for a gray long-haired cat with a white smudge on its nose. She called everyone she knew. Every cat she found was either too young or too old, not gray enough or too gray, or had the white spot on its paws instead of its nose, or no white spot at all. Time was running out. She knew that no matter how many toys or presents Santa left under the tree, if Whiskers wasn't there, it was going to be a miserable Christmas.

We had a big holiday planned, as usual. Dad was coming in from California, and Grandma and Grandpa Gregory and Grammy Burke, and Uncle Paul and Uncle Derrick were coming from Washington, and, of course, Aunt Bridget and Aunt Lindsay and their families were all coming for Christmas dinner. They were all bringing food and presents and it should have been the best Christmas ever. But believe me, as Christmas

Eve arrived and there was still no sign of Whiskers, there was no joy in Whoville that year.

But you know my mom. She is unstoppable. With half the state of Maryland and most of D.C. on the lookout for a gray cat with a white nose, she got lucky at the last minute. When I came downstairs on Christmas morning, there she was waiting at the bottom of the stairs, all backlit by the Christmas tree, with Whiskers in her arms.

I was ecstatic. I ran down the stairs and snatched up Whiskers, hugging him and covering him with kisses . . . and he screamed and hissed and scratched me on the arm. I tried to forgive him for being in such a bad mood, but even I could tell there was something different about him. Just then there was a knock on the back door and Aunt Lindsay came in with a big cardboard box in her arms, calling, "Merry Christmas everyone! You won't believe who I found waiting outside my door this morning!"

My mom looked as though she was about to have a conniption, waving both arms and shushing Aunt Lindsay, and twisting her face this way and that, but it didn't matter, because just as Aunt Lindsay set the box on the floor and a fuzzy gray cat with a spot on its nose jumped out, I realized that the spot on Whiskers' nose—or at least what I thought was a spot—was flaking off. Mom had used white typewriter eraser liquid to paint a spot on the cat's nose, and it hadn't worked very well. Before I could even recover from the blow that Whiskers had not, in fact, come home for Christmas, Aunt Bridget was at the front door with yet another gray cat she pretended to have found hiding under her porch. At least this one had a real white nose, but it was not Whiskers. The fact that it was a girl cat should have been a dead giveaway.

The Christmas tree was piled up with gifts from Santa Claus, but I couldn't have cared less. I now had not one, but three cats, even though none of them was Whiskers, and I didn't know whether to cry or celebrate. Before I could decide, Daddy was at the door, loaded down with presents all the way from California . . . including a box wrapped in gingerbread-man Christmas paper with holes punched in the side and a fuzzy gray kitten screaming to be let out. Grammy Burke came with a prissy gray Persian who hissed at everybody and peed on Mom's rug, and Grandma and Grandpa Gregory claimed Santa had left a big gray cat under their tree with a note that they should deliver it to me. And by the time Uncle Paul and Uncle Derrick arrived, I didn't even have to guess what was in the wicker basket they carried.

We ended up with five cats and three kittens on Christmas morning and my mom was frantic. After all, she had a lot more to explain than just how a half dozen Whiskers imposters had ended up on our doorstep. She had told me Santa could only find our house if everyone was in the Christmas picture, remember? But Whiskers had not been in the picture and Santa clearly couldn't have been more pleased with me. Oh, what a tangled web we weave when first we practice to deceive.

I sat on the floor with cats crawling all over me while Mom and Dad and the two Grandmas tried very hard *not* to say ugly things to each other, and Uncle Derrick and Uncle Paul argued over whether to put the plaid sofa or the pink divan in the living room of the doll house Santa had brought me, and everyone tried to pretend it was a perfectly normal Christmas. Which, for our house, I suppose it was. I was sitting there in the middle of all that chaos, presents still unopened, cats yowling and adults hissing and spitting at each other when I swear I heard sleigh bells. Really. I ran through the house and threw open the back door and sitting on the stoop, skinny and bedraggled-looking, his red bow in tatters but the jingle bells still intact, was Whiskers. The real one.

Apparently he had gotten locked in a neighbor's storage shed the day he ran away, and had been living off of mice and bugs ever since. When the neighbor went out on Christmas Eve to get the bike he'd been hiding for his little boy for Christmas, Whiskers escaped and made his way home.

It was a Christmas miracle. And one I'll never, ever get tired of telling people about.

Chapter Twelve

In Which a Star Appears in the East

"Of course," said Cici, sipping her wine, "the real miracle was that we were able to find good homes for eight cats."

Even Lindsay was smiling by this time. "And that you didn't kill any of us before dinner."

"But the important thing is that Mom learned her lesson," Lori said. "She was trying to protect me from the truth about Whiskers, and look at all the trouble it caused. And all the time what she thought she was protecting me from wasn't even the truth at all."

Ida Mae gave a curt shake of her head. "Craziest thing I ever did hear of. All them cats in the house."

Bridget said thoughtfully, "This place could use a cat."

Cici gave her a hard look. "Don't start."

Lori said sagely, "You know what the moral of the story is, don't you?"

"That you," declared Paul, lifting his glass to her, "were the most adored child who ever lived. Do you know how many people were out breaking their necks on Christmas Eve to avoid breaking your heart?"

Lori beamed with satisfaction. "That's true. And all that love and devotion is exactly why I grew to be as spectacular as I am. But that's not the moral of the story." She leaned forward in the rocker, her expression earnest. "The moral of the story is that you can't make a miracle. Sometimes you just have to wait for it."

Cici came over to her daughter, leaned down, and kissed her hair. "You're still the most adored child who ever lived," she said. "Now, get out of my chair."

Lindsay smiled at them both with wry and tender affection. "You know something?" she said. "I think I'll get cleaned up and change my clothes while I'm waiting for my miracle. Ida Mae is right. It's Christmas Eve, and I'm not going to the dinner table smelling like a wet horse."

"And this is why we have gas appliances," Bridget said cheerfully, "Ida Mae, put the bread pudding in the oven and start warming up the gravy. It's time for dinner."

"Who cares if the lights are out?" Derrick added. "Candlelight is more glamorous anyway."

"Maybe I'll put on a dress," Cici said.

"Oh-oh," Paul said. "You know that means I have to wear a tie."

"And who knows?" Lori said, rising to go in the house. "By the time we're ready, Noah could be here."

"Right," said Cici, but as she met Bridget's eyes they both were struggling to hold their smiles. "Who knows?"

Kathy said, "You don't have the first idea where we are, do you?"

Noah wanted to insist that of course he did, that they couldn't be more than a mile or two from home, and he knew he probably should have lied because it was better than telling the truth. But he just wasn't up to it. "It's pretty dark," he said. There were farmhouses and trailer parks all over this part of the countryside. They should have started seeing lights by now.

Kathy shook her head in slow dismay. "Could this Christmas get any better?" she muttered. "This is what I get for following a seventeen year old kid across the woods just because he says he knows where he's going." She stumbled and almost fell. "Are we even on the road anymore?"

Noah scowled and hunched his shoulders. "You want to turn back, feel free."

"Hey." She caught his arm and he jerked it away. She closed her fingers on his elbow, harder this time, and he stopped and turned to her. It was too dark to see her face, but he didn't have to. She was breathing hard.

"Listen," she said. "This is crazy. The further we walk, the more lost we're getting. We need to just stop, right now, and wait for morning."

The thing was, she was probably right. It was too dark to see his hand in front of his face, and who knew how far off course they'd traveled. . . . If they'd even been on course in the first place. There was no sign of civilization, and no sign of getting closer to it. He could tell she was tired; so was he, and he hadn't just spent the last eight months in a hospital. He stood looking at her for a long moment, thinking about it. Knowing what he should do, and knowing, all the time, what he was going to do.

He swung his saddlebags off his shoulder, unbuckled a pocket, and felt around inside until he came up with the two candy bars. He put them in her hand. "Here," he said. "They're a little squashed, but they ought to hold you until morning. I'll send somebody for you as soon as I find a phone."

She stared at the candy in her hand. "You can't just go off by yourself."

"Have to," he replied, and slung the saddlebags back on his shoulder. "My folks are waiting for me."

She tried to peer through the darkness to make out his face. "I thought you said your folks were dead."

He shrugged. "My mom and dad are," he said. "But my real family—my real mom—they're at home now, expecting me, and I told them I would be back, so I will be."

She was silent for a moment, and when she spoke again her voice had softened, "You're a pretty lucky kid, to have a family worth going through all this for."

He replied simply, "I know."

She took a breath, straightened her shoulders, and handed one of the candy bars back to him. "So," she said, unwrapping her own candy. "Which way?"

Noah looked around for a moment, straining for something, anything, that would give him a clue. There was nothing but black night, black lumps, black tree trunks as far as he could see. He hated to admit it, but even this brief stop had gotten him turned around, and he didn't even know in which direction he'd been going originally. Not that it mattered, since he'd probably been going the wrong way the whole time.

Then Kathy caught her breath. He heard her say reverently, "Holy sh—I mean, holy cow."

He frowned in surprise because he could actually see the faintest outline of the shape of her face in the darkness. She appeared to be staring at something over his shoulder. He turned, and he stared too.

In the distance a cone of light had appeared, illuminating the tops of trees and the underside of low-hanging clouds, reflecting off the dense, humid atmosphere and spreading particles of pale radiance over the sky. For a long time, they just stood there, staring, and then a slow grin spread over Noah's face. "Looks good to me," he said, and they started walking toward the light.

"Can you believe that?" Bridget said, switching off her flashlight as she entered the circle of lantern light and candlelight that was the foyer of Ladybug Farm. Through the open screen door the sounds of chugging engines, crackling radios and industry followed her. "The transformer at the end of our driveway is one of the ones that controls this whole part of the county. They can't turn any of the power back on until they change out some switch or something. They really appreciated the sandwiches and coffee, Ida Mae," she added, "and they thought the cookies were fabulous."

Ida Mae gave a grunt of acknowledgement and muttered something about feeding every stray in the county as she went back to the kitchen.

Cici peered out toward the road, where spotlights and the sound of shouted orders indicated the presence of the power company workers. "Maybe we *did* take out the grid when we plugged in the lights," she said, sounding concerned.

Lindsay looked over her shoulder. "Those guys are heroes," she said. "Working in the dark like that on Christmas Eve. They deserve more than sandwiches and coffee."

"I invited them back to the house for eggnog,"

Derrick said, "but I think that's against company policy."

Dinner had been delayed again while Bridget and Ida Mae made sandwiches for the crew, and Bridget and Derrick drove to deliver them. But everyone had showered and changed out of their work clothes, and the house was once again redolent with the aromas of the coming feast. Paul lit the candles on the table while Bridget and Derrick brought in platters of sliced turkey and dressing, bowls of vegetables and a basket of hot rolls. Cici poured the wine. Paul snapped another picture on his cell phone, but it came out a little blurry with the candlelight.

Lori came into the dining room, having changed into a sundress and tied back her hair, rubbing her hands together eagerly. "I'm starved! This is the latest we've ever had dinner, isn't it? It's practically Continental. Everything smells incredible."

Lindsay stood near the doorway, surveying the scene—the candlelight glowing on the soft patina of the silver and flickering on the crystal, shining in the gentle smiles of her friends and dancing on the dark windows. The table was set for a feast, and the smells of Christmas filled the air. She let her eyes linger on the empty place setting for only a moment, and then she moved to the table and took up her wine glass. "A toast," she said, lifting her glass. "To friends and family, near and far. God bless us every one."

There was the clink of glasses around the table, the murmur of "hear, hear", and then the scraping of chairs as Lori declared with enthusiasm, "Now, let's eat."

Lindsay laughed and allowed Paul to pull out her chair for her. "All right, then, let's eat!"

Behind them, a voice said, "Y'all aren't going to start without me, are you?"

Lindsay dropped her glass and whirled, but her cry of joy was lost in the clamor that followed.

"Noah!"

"Where've you been?"

"We've been worried sick!"

"What happened to you?"

"Oh, it doesn't matter, it doesn't matter, he's home now!"

Everyone descended on Noah, hugging him, clapping him on the back, almost knocking him down with their enthusiasm. He tried to laugh it off, but he was too tired, and too relieved and glad to even pretend to be embarrassed. He hugged everyone back, even Lori.

Lindsay stepped back, holding his shoulders, peering through the candlelight at the scratches and smudges on his face. "What happened?" she demanded, her voice hoarse. "Are you all right?"

He shrugged a little. "A little accident, that's all. That helmet you gave me worked great, though."

Lindsay's hand dropped to her heart.

Noah glanced over his shoulder to the woman who, in all the excitement, they had only just begun to realize was behind him, half hidden in the shadows. He drew her forward. "Everybody, this is Kathy," he said. He added with a touch of importance in his voice, "She was a soldier in Iraq. This," he said, and now his tone was firm with pride, "is my family."

They swarmed in on her, just as he knew they would, welcoming her and drawing her into the dining room.

"Come in, come in, join us."

"We were just about to sit down to dinner."

"Let me pour you a glass of wine."

Kathy raised both hands in protest, looking uncertain and overwhelmed. "Um, really," she said, "I'm a mess. I wrecked my car and . . . I mean, I just came in to use the phone."

"Don't be ridiculous. Of course you'll stay."

"Don't worry about a thing, we'll see about your car as soon as we all have something to eat."

"Who do you need to call, honey? You must be exhausted."

"Do you have any place to stay tonight? We have plenty of room. And just wait until you taste Ida Mae's Christmas morning pancakes."

Kathy looked at Noah, her eyes wide with cautious disbelief. Noah looked back at her and grinned.

"Please," she said, glancing around at the others, "I'm filthy. I couldn't possibly . . ."

"Oh you poor thing." Bridget slipped an arm around her waist. "What must you have been through? Come with me, I'll show you where you can clean up. I hope you don't mind lantern light. It's all we have right now . . ." She led her away.

Lindsay didn't seem to be able to stop looking at Noah, and it was Cici who said, "Noah, what happened? We've been just sick with worry."

He said, as casually as possible, "I ran into a skid on a back road on the way back from Staunton. I broke my phone. That girl, Kathy, her car went into a ditch. We've been walking since this afternoon."

Paul said in astonishment, "Walking? All this time?"

Noah nodded, a little abashed. "It got dark on us sooner than I expected, and my flashlight died. We wouldn't have made it at all except for those guys working with the spotlights at the end of the driveway. Did you know that's the only light you can see anywhere around in this whole part of the county?"

Paul looked at Derrick. Derrick looked at Cici. Cici looked at Lindsay, and Lindsay looked at Lori, and not one of them could find a single thing to say.

Noah turned to Lindsay. He lowered his voice

a little and said, "Listen, I'm sorry you were worried." He dropped his eyes. "I guess I screwed up. It's just—well, it was Christmas and all, and I wanted to get you something special. I got a present for you, it wasn't much, but it got busted in the accident. So I'm sorry."

Lindsay wrapped her hand around his arm, and pressed her cheek against his shoulder. "You did get me something special," she told him. Her voice sounded thick, and at the same time, light. Her smile was radiant in the candlelight. "You brought me the best Christmas present ever."

Cici blotted her eyes with the back of her hand. Lori put her arm around her mother's waist. Derrick covered Paul's hand with his.

Ida Mae stood at the door to the kitchen, her arms across her chest. "Are y'all gonna eat, or what?"

Cici sniffed and swiped again at her eyes and turned to Ida Mae, beaming. "We've got company," she said. "Set another place, will you? And Noah." She spun back to him. "Run get cleaned up. We're starving and, to tell the truth, I'm not sure I can stay awake much longer. Lord help us all, I don't think I can *ever* go through another night like this one."

There was a faint knock from the front of the house, and a voice called, "Excuse me? Ma'am?"

"I'll check it out," Lori said, but everyone, including Noah, followed her to the front door.

A man in a power company uniform and a hard hat was at the screen door. "I brought back your thermos," he said, holding it up. "And your basket. The men wanted me to tell you thanks again."

"Young man!" exclaimed Paul, rushing to the door. "Come in, come in!"

"You saved our lives!" Lindsay cried. She caught his hand and pulled him inside.

Cici said, "Do you have any idea what you've done?"

And Lori declared, "A miracle, that's what it is. A real miracle."

"What we're all trying to say," said Derrick, pumping his hand enthusiastically, "is thank you. Thank you for service above and beyond the call of duty!"

"Well actually," the young man replied, looking confused, "I'm on call for holidays and week-ends through January fifteenth. What I wanted to tell you was we've about got you back online, and you should have power any minute now."

With a hum and a flicker, the lights came back on around the house. The young man glanced around, smiling. "Well, there you go."

The Christmas tree sprang to life. The window wreaths glowed, the porch and garden sparkled, the archways were illuminated with tiny lights. It was so beautiful, and so welcome, that everyone burst into spontaneous applause. Paul whipped out his cell phone and started snapping pictures.

Behind them, an awed voice said, "Oh, my. Will you look at that?"

The young man in the power company uniform turned sharply, staring at the newcomer. His throat worked convulsively for a moment, and he seemed unable to speak. Finally he managed, "Kathy?"

Noah was the first to notice the expression in her eyes as she turned to look at him, the way the color drained from her face and her hand went to her throat. She whispered, "Roger."

She broke away from Bridget and took a couple of steps toward him. He pushed passed Derrick and Paul, and everyone in the room fell into puzzled silence, intent upon the drama in the making as he strode across the room and stood in front of Kathy, staring at her.

She looked up at him with tears glittering on her lashes. Her voice was broken. "I tried to find you. I went to your house . . ."

"I got this job." His voice was hoarse. He kept staring. "I haven't lived there since summer. I wrote you a couple of thousand e-mails."

She whispered, "I didn't think you'd want me."

He pushed her hair away from her face. He looked at her for a long, long time. And then he said softly, "Oh, baby. Why wouldn't I want you?" and he pulled her into his arms.

Noah nodded, and a slow, rather smug grin turned up the corner of his lips. "Nice," he murmured.

Lori cast a meaningful, big-eyed glance from him to the embracing couple and back again. "What . . . ?"

He gave an elaborate shrug, clearly reveling in the secret he would share at his own leisure. "Long story," he said.

Kathy broke away just then, laughing, her cheeks wet with happy tears. "I'm sorry, everyone," she said. "We're being rude. You don't even know us, and this is such a surprise . . . This is my—"

She stumbled over the word and looked at Roger, but before he could answer the unspoken question in her eyes, Noah supplied easily, "Fiancé. It's her fiancé. Right?"

Roger said, without taking his eyes off her, "Right. Kathy, I can't believe it. I can't believe it's you. How did you . . . ?"

"Long story," she replied, beaming.

He swept a glance around the room, barely focusing on any of them, and said, "I'm sorry, we don't mean to interrupt your holiday. I didn't know Kathy was here. I've been looking for her . . ."

"I've been looking for you," she whispered.

It was Bridget who recovered herself first. "What a lovely reunion!" she exclaimed softly, pressing her hands together in delight. "We'd be honored if you both would be our guests for dinner tonight."

Roger glanced around, and by the distracted look on his face it was clear he wasn't certain who had spoken. "Thank you ma'am. That's kind. But I, that is we . . ." He looked helplessly at Kathy, "Would you walk outside with me for a minute?"

Kathy smiled. "Well, I've walked this far, what's a few more steps?"

Paul surreptitiously snapped a photo of them as they left the room. "Now *that*," he declared happily, "is a Christmas story."

"The best one yet," agreed Derrick.

"Wait until you hear the rest of it," Noah said.

From the doorway, Ida Mae demanded again, "Are y'all gonna eat or do you want me to feed this to the dog?"

"We're coming," called Cici.

Paul said, "Wait." He held up his cell phone camera. "This calls for a picture. Everyone, scrunch in close together in front of the tree. Look this way."

They all turned toward the camera, and then Noah exclaimed suddenly, "Hold on a minute." He looked at Lindsay. "I just remembered, I got you something after all."

The others waited, trying to hold the pose, while

he scrambled in his saddlebags. He returned with a sprig of mistletoe, which he held over Lindsay's head. Lindsay looked up at him, laughing.

"Merry Christmas, Mom," he said, and kissed her cheek.

Paul snapped the picture.

It was perfect.

Recipes from Ladybug Farm

— *A Companion Cookbook* —

On Ladybug Farm, something is always cooking. Whether it's strawberry jam in the spring, blueberry scones in the summer, Brunswick stew in the autumn or Ida Mae's fruitcakes in the winter, the halls of the grand old mansion are always redolent of delicious flavors, and the kitchen is the heart of the home.

Based on her beloved Ladybug Farm series, the author of *A Year on Ladybug Farm*, *At Home on Ladybug Farm* and *Love Letters from Ladybug Farm* has put together this collection of most-requested recipes for her readers. Using fresh, seasonal ingredients with a dash of Southern flair, this collection is sure to be a favorite of amateur cooks both on and off Ladybug Farm.

Table of Contents

Christmas

Introduction

One of the first things readers always mention to me about the Ladybug Farm books is the food—how often it is described throughout the books, and how wonderful it all sounds. I'm often asked why food plays such an important part in the texture of the books, and for me the answer is simple: you can't write a book about women without also writing about food. Women are natural nurturers, and they do most of their nurturing —as well as their socializing—through food.

Don't expect this to be a traditional cookbook. I've organized it according to seasons, not logic, because when you eat what you grow—like Cici, Bridget and Lindsay learned to do—you make what you can out of what you have . . . and in the case of the ladies of Ladybug Farm, sometimes that's pretty spectacular. Like Ida Mae, I am an intuitive cook—a dash of this, a pinch of that—so feel free to experiment with these recipes and if you come up with something you like better, let me know.

Meantime, pull up a rocking chair on the front porch, pour yourself a glass of wine, and take your time browsing through the kitchen of Ladybug Farm. I hope you find something you love!

—*Donna Ball*

The Kitchen of Ladybug Farm

Bridget walked to the center of the enormous room, drew in a breath, and pressed both hands to her cheeks, turning full circle. "Oh, my goodness," she said.

The floor was paved in brick worn smooth by time, and the antique brick on the walls was oiled to a sheen. There was a raised cooking fireplace at one end of the enormous room where they could imagine placing a downy sofa and a couple of chairs for cozy winter evenings. The center island was soapstone, and the counter tops were tiled in cottage white and delft blue. The back splash behind the deep farmer's sink was a mural in the blue willow pattern. There were two big stoves, two dishwashers, a giant refrigerator and an upright freezer. "Obviously, the kitchen has been upgraded over the years, and the appliances are industrial grade," Maggie said. "The Blackwells did a lot of entertaining in their prime."

Bridget touched one of the stoves reverently. "Oh my God," she said. "This is a Viking."

"Bet you could whip up a casserole or two on that, huh Bridge?" said Lindsay with a grin.

"Of course all appliances are included," Maggie said. "And there's a butler's pantry."

Bridget dashed off to explore it, and in a moment they heard a muffled squeal of delight.

"I hate the tile," Cici said, but she was grinning too. It had been a long time since either of them had seen their friend this happy.

In a moment Bridget returned, breathless with excitement. "Unbelievable," she said. "The silverware drawers are lined with blue velvet. There's a pie safe with a lock! And just outside there's a walled herb garden. Some of the herbs are still growing. There's a rosemary bush as big as a tree!"

Maggie was looking very pleased with herself, and Cici knew what she was thinking, what any real estate agent worth her commission would think: the kitchen sells the house.

—A Year on Ladybug Farm

Spring

Strawberry Season

On Ladybug Farm, the best part of spring is strawberry season. The sunny hills are covered with vines, every basket, bowl and pot in the kitchen is filled with fruit, and for weeks at a time the entire house smells like strawberries, strawberries, strawberries.

Bridget's Strawberry Cobbler

- 1 cup flour
- 1 cup sugar
- 1 stick butter, softened
- 3 cups strawberries, hulled and sliced
- ¼ cup sugar
- 1 teaspoon vanilla extract
- 2 tablespoons cornstarch

Preheat oven to 350.

Mix together flour, 1 cup sugar and butter in food processor or with a pastry cutter. In a separate bowl, toss strawberries with ¼ cup sugar, vanilla and cornstarch. Butter a deep 8- or 9-inch casserole dish and pour in strawberry mixture. Top with crumbled flour mixture. Place on baking sheet to catch spill-over, and bake until golden and bubbly, about 30 minutes.

Serve warm with whipped cream or vanilla ice cream.

Strawberry Trifle

- 1 angel food cake (store-bought is fine)
- 1 quart fresh strawberries, sliced
- 1½ cups sugar, divided
- 8 ounces cream cheese, softened
- 8 ounces sour cream
- ¼ cup plus 2 tablespoons amaretto, divided

Slice fresh strawberries and cover with 1 cup sugar. Add 2 tablespoons amaretto. Stir gently and let strawberries sit at room temperature until a syrup forms, about half an hour.

Tear angel food cake into cubes; set aside.

Mix sour cream, cream cheese and ½ cup sugar with ¼ cup amaretto at medium speed on a mixer until smooth, about 3 minutes.

Line a trifle bowl (or any large, clear glass bowl) with ⅓ of the cubed angel food cake. Pour ⅓ of the strawberry mixture over it. Top with ½ the cream cheese mixture, spreading to edges as evenly as possible. Layer ⅓ of the cake cubes, top with ⅓ strawberry mixture. Spread remaining cream cheese on top. Top with remaining cake cubes, add remaining strawberry mixture. Cover and let sit overnight. Before serving, decorate with fresh sliced strawberries.

Ida Mae says . . . Don't even bother with those cardboard strawberries you get from the store in the winter. Anything worth making is worth making fresh.

Bridget says . . . Sometimes I use strawberries frozen out of our garden.

Strawberry Muffins

- ¼ cup butter, melted
- ½ cup milk
- 1 egg
- ½ teaspoon salt
- 2 teaspoons baking powder
- ½ cup sugar
- 1¾ cups all-purpose flour
- 1 cup chopped strawberries

Preheat oven to 375.

In a small bowl, combine butter, sugar, milk, and egg. Beat lightly. In a large bowl, mix flour, salt, and baking powder together. Toss in chopped strawberries and stir to coat with flour. Pour in milk mixture and stir until well blended.

Fill 8 well-oiled muffin cups ⅔ full. Bake at 375 for 25 minutes, or until the tops bounce back from the touch. Cool 10 minutes and remove from pans.

Strawberry Pancakes

- 1 large egg
- 1 cup milk
- 1 teaspoon vanilla extract
- 2 tablespoons unsalted butter, melted, plus more for serving
- 1 cup strawberries
- 1¼ cups all-purpose flour
- 2 tablespoons granulated sugar
- 3 teaspoons baking powder
- ½ teaspoon salt

Strawberry syrup, for serving (recipe follows)

In a blender or food processor, blend the wet ingredients together with the strawberries. Add the dry ingredients in thirds, blending after each addition.

Pour the batter onto a hot, well-buttered griddle ¼ cup at a time. Turn when bubbles break on the top, 2-3 minutes. Cook until golden brown, about 2 minutes more. Serve with butter and strawberry syrup.

Strawberry Syrup

- 1 cup strawberries, sliced
- ½ cup sugar
- 1 teaspoon lemon juice

Puree all ingredients together in a blender. Pour into small saucepan and bring to boil over low heat. Boil and stir for one minute. Strain through fine sieve or cheesecloth. Serve warm with pancakes.

Strawberry Shortcake

- 2 cups sliced strawberries
- ½ cup sugar

For cake:
- 1 cup white sugar
- ½ cup butter
- 2 eggs
- 2 teaspoons vanilla extract
- 1½ cups all-purpose flour
- 2 teaspoons baking powder
- ½ cup milk

For topping:
- 1 cup heavy whipping cream
- ½ cup sugar
- 1 teaspoon vanilla extract

Preheat oven to 350. Grease and flour a 9-inch round pan.

Mix strawberries and sugar together; set aside.

In a medium bowl, cream together the sugar and butter. Beat in the eggs, one at a time, then stir in the vanilla. Combine flour and baking powder, add to the creamed mixture and mix well. Finally stir in the milk until batter is smooth. Pour or spoon batter into the prepared pan.

Bake for 30 to 40 minutes in the preheated oven, until cake springs back to the touch. Let cake cool for 10 minutes, remove from pan.

Cool completely.

Meanwhile, whip cream until stiff peaks form, sprinkling in the sugar a tablespoon at a time. Stir in vanilla. Refrigerate.

Slice cake in half horizontally. Place one half on serving platter and spoon one half of the strawberries on top, allowing some of the juice to soak into the cake. Top with half the whipped cream. Add the other half of the cake, top with remaining strawberries and whipped cream.

Strawberry Coulis

- 6 cups strawberries, fresh or frozen
- 1 cup granulated sugar
- ¼ cup port wine or frambroise

Combine all the ingredients in a saucepan and bring the mix to a boil. Once it is boiling and the sugar has been dissolved, remove from heat and transfer the mixture to a blender.

Add wine or framboise and blend until it is very smooth, and then pass the sauce through a mesh strainer to remove the seeds. Serve as a topping for ice cream, cheesecake, or pound cake.

Creamy Strawberry Salad Dressing

- 1 cup fresh strawberries
- 1 clove garlic, minced
- 2 teaspoons honey
- Juice of one lemon
- ½ cup mayonnaise
- ¼ teaspoon salt

Mix in blender until creamy. Store in tightly covered container in refrigerator for up to 3 days.

Bridget's Pan Bread

- ½ cup butter, very soft
- 2 cups flour
- 1 teaspoon soda
- ½ teaspoon salt
- ⅔ cup buttermilk
- 1 tablespoon chopped fresh rosemary
- ½ cup shredded cheddar cheese

Preheat oven to 425.

Mix together flour, soda and salt in a bowl. Cut in butter with a pastry blender, fork or your fingers. Add buttermilk, rosemary and cheddar and blend with spoon just until mixed. Turn into a well-greased 8x8 skillet or cake pan and bake at 425 20-25 minutes. Serve warm with butter.

A Special Luncheon Menu

Minted Asparagus Soup

Four Cheese Soufflé
with Roasted Pepper Puree

Mini-Scones stuffed with
Cherry Cream Cheese

Wild Dandelion Salad
with Raspberry Vinaigrette

Cheese Biscuits and Pinot Noir Jam

—Love Letters From Ladybug Farm

Minted Asparagus Soup

- 3 cups prepared chicken broth
- 2 bunches fresh asparagus, tender parts only
- Juice of one lemon
- I cup chopped fresh mint
- 1 cup cream
- Salt to taste
- 3 slices smoked bacon, fried and crumbled
- Rosemary olive oil for garnish

Discard the woody ends of the asparagus and chop the green tender tips into 1-inch pieces.

Bring chicken broth to a simmer and add asparagus; cook just until al dente, about 5 minutes. Reserve 1 tablespoon chopped mint for garnish, and add the remainder to the asparagus. Stir in cream and continue to cook just until warm (do not boil!), about 2 minutes. Remove from heat. Add lemon juice and transfer to blender (or use an immersion blender). Blend until smooth. Taste and salt if necessary.

Chill. Just before serving, top with a drizzle of rosemary-infused olive oil and a sprinkle of crumbled bacon.

Four Cheese Soufflé
with Roasted Red Pepper Puree

- ¼ cup butter
- ¼ cup all-purpose flour
- 1¼ cups milk
- ¼ teaspoon cayenne
- ¼ teaspoon salt
- ½ cup shredded sharp cheddar cheese
- ½ cup pepper jack cheese
- ½ cup Gruyere cheese
- ½ cup Swiss cheese
- 6 large eggs, separated
- ¼ teaspoon cream of tartar

Generously butter a 2-quart soufflé dish or 6 1- to 1¼-cup soufflé dishes; if using small ones, set them about 2 inches apart in a 10x15-inch baking pan.

In a 2- to 3-quart pan over medium heat, melt ¼ cup butter. Add flour and stir until mixture is smooth and bubbly. Stir in milk, cayenne, and salt, stirring continuously until sauce boils and thickens, 3 to 4 minutes. Remove from heat.

Add cheese and stir until melted. Add egg yolks and stir until the mixture is blended and smooth.

In a large bowl beat egg whites and cream of tartar on high speed until stiff peaks form. Fold a third of the cheese sauce into whites until well blended. Add remaining sauce and gently fold in just until blended.

Scrape the batter into the prepared soufflé dish. Bake in a 375 oven until top is golden to deep brown and cracks look fairly dry, 25 to 30 minutes for large soufflé, 15 to 20 minutes for small ones. Serve immediately on a bed of warm roasted red pepper puree.

Red Pepper Puree

- 2 large red bell peppers, roasted and chopped
- ¼ cup extra-virgin olive oil
- 1½ teaspoons fresh lemon juice
- ½ teaspoon salt

Place all ingredients in a blender and puree until smooth.

Mini-Scones
Stuffed with Cherry Cream Cheese

- 2 cups flour
- ¼ cup sugar
- 3 teaspoons baking powder
- ½ teaspoon salt
- 8 tablespoons chilled butter, cut into pieces
- ½ cup dried cherries, chopped
- 1 egg
- ½ cup heavy cream
- 2 teaspoons almond flavoring
- Granulated sugar for sprinkling

Preheat oven to 350 and lightly grease a baking sheet.

Combine flour, sugar, baking powder, and salt. Work in the butter in small pieces using a pastry cutter or food processor until the mixture resembles pea-size crumbs.

Add dried cherries to flour mixture. Mix to coat.

In a small bowl, combine egg, heavy cream and almond extract. Whisk to combine. Add to flour mixture. Using a fork, combine to form large clumps.

Turn the dough out onto a lightly floured surface and knead 5-6 times. Roll into a 9-inch square, cut into 1-inch circles with a cookie cutter, miniature biscuit cutter, or medium bottle cap.

Place on greased baking sheet and sprinkle each scone lightly with sugar. Bake until the scones are golden, about 18 minutes.

Let the scones cool until warm enough to handle while preparing the filling.

Cherry Cream Cheese Filling

- 3 ounces cream cheese, softened
- ¼ cup confectioners' sugar
- ¼ teaspoon almond flavoring
- ½ cup finely chopped dried cherries

Mix all ingredients together in food processor until smooth. Fill a pastry bag with a medium tip and pipe the filling into the center of each scone. Alternatively, you can split each scone in half, pile the filling on the bottom, and top with the other half.

Wild Dandelion Salad
with Raspberry Vinaigrette

- ½ cup toasted walnuts
- 3 slices cooked bacon, broken, not crumbled
- 4-5 cups chopped new dandelion leaves
- 1 hardboiled egg, sliced
- ¼ cup chopped spring onion

Toss dandelion leaves with bacon, onion, and toasted walnuts. Plate and drizzle raspberry vinaigrette (recipe follows) over each serving. Top each with decorative slices of egg.

Raspberry Vinaigrette

- ½ cup extra-virgin olive oil
- 2 tablespoons honey
- 1 tablespoon Dijon mustard
- 4 tablespoons red wine vinegar
- 1 teaspoon fresh lemon juice
- Salt and pepper to taste
- ½ cup fresh raspberries

Combine all ingredients in blender and blend until emulsified. Makes about 1¼ cups.

Cheese Biscuits

- 2 cups all-purpose flour
- 2½ teaspoons baking powder
- ½ teaspoon salt
- ½ cup butter
- 1½ cups shredded cheddar cheese
- ⅔ cup milk

Preheat the oven to 425. Lightly grease a baking sheet.

In a mixing bowl, combine flour, salt and baking powder. Cut in butter with a pastry cutter until crumbly. Stir in the cheese and milk. Mix with a fork until the dough comes together and forms a ball.

Turn the dough out onto a lightly floured board and knead 5-6 times. Roll the dough out to a 1-inch thickness. Cut with a 2-inch biscuit cutter.

Bake for 12-15 minutes or until light golden brown. Brush lightly with melted butter as soon as biscuits are removed from oven.

Serve warm with butter or an exotic wine jam like cherry or pinot noir.

Easter Dinner

The Easter table was spectacular. The wine stain
had been removed from the white damask
tablecloth through some miracle of baking soda
and lemon juice. A three-tiered silver candelabra
bearing a dozen snow white candles sent sparks of
light dancing across every glass, plate, spoon and
mirror in the room, and gave off enough heat that
everyone was grateful for the breeze that billowed
the lace curtains at the open window. The ham,
beautifully browned and glistening with honey
glaze, rested on a bed of fresh parsley and red
spiced apple rings, and was surrounded—in
homage to a tradition only Ida Mae understood
and would not deign to explain—by bright yellow
deviled eggs sprinkled with paprika. Bowls of
garden fresh peas and carrots, roasted new
potatoes, and fluffy sweet potato casserole flanked
the ham platter, accompanied by buttered corn
from last year's garden, a pineapple-cheese
casserole that was Ida Mae's specialty, and a
basket of fragrant homemade rolls. The table was
set with Cici's Havilland china and Bridget's

Baccarat crystal and starched white linen napkins. At each place setting was a bright yellow daffodil in a silver bud vase, courtesy of Lindsay, who collected bud vases.

Having the preacher to dinner was not something that happened every day.

—At Home on Ladybug Farm

Easter Ham

- 1 (8- to 10-pound) smoked ham, bone-in, skin on
- Kosher salt and freshly ground black pepper
- 1 cup (2 sticks) unsalted butter, cut in chunks
- 1 cup orange juice
- ½ cup bourbon
- 1 cup honey
- 1 cup water
- ¼ teaspoon whole cloves

Preheat the oven to 300.

Put the ham in a large roasting pan, fat-side up. Using a sharp knife, score the ham with cuts across the skin, about 2 inches apart and ½-inch deep. Cut diagonally down the slashes to form a diamond pattern; season the meat generously with salt and pepper. Place ham in oven.

Melt together in a small saucepan over medium heat the butter, orange juice, honey, water, bourbon and cloves. Slowly cook the liquid down to a syrupy glaze; this should take about 30 to 40 minutes.

Bake ham for 2 hours; remove and pour glaze over it. Return to oven and continue to bake for 2 hours, basting with the juices every 30 minutes.

Deviled Eggs

- 6 hard-cooked eggs, peeled and cut lengthwise
- ¼ cup mayonnaise
- ½ teaspoon Dijon mustard powder
- ⅛ teaspoon salt
- ¼ teaspoon ground black pepper
- Paprika for garnish

Pop out the egg yolks to a small bowl and mash with a fork. Add mayonnaise, mustard powder, salt and pepper and mix thoroughly. Fill the empty egg white shells with the mixture and sprinkle lightly with paprika.

Pineapple Cheese Casserole

- 2 (15 ounce) cans pineapple chunks, drained
- 1 cup white sugar
- 1 cup all-purpose flour
- 2½ cups shredded sharp cheddar cheese
- 25 buttery round crackers, crumbled
- ½ cup melted butter

Preheat oven to 350.

Place pineapple in the bottom of a buttered 2-quart casserole dish.

In a small bowl, stir together the sugar, flour and cheese. Add to casserole dish.

Sprinkle crackers over the top of pineapple and cheese mixture. Pour melted butter over the top and bake for 30 minutes.

Sweet Potato Casserole

- 3 cups baked, mashed sweet potatoes
- 1 cup brown sugar
- 2 eggs, lightly beaten
- 1 teaspoon vanilla
- ½ cup heavy cream
- ½ cup melted butter

Mix ingredients with a hand mixer just until combined. Pour into well-buttered 2-quart casserole dish. Add topping (below).

Topping:
- ½ cup brown sugar
- ⅓ cup flour
- ⅓ cup melted butter
- 1 cup chopped pecans

Mix together with fork until crumbly and sprinkle over the top of the sweet potatoes. Bake at 350 for 30 to 40 minutes, until hot and browned.

Ida Mae says . . . Bake your sweet potatoes at 400 for one hour. Baking brings out the sweetness.

Summer

Blueberry Season

Blueberry season on Ladybug Farm is heralded by warm bright days, cool nights, and the rows of waxy-leaved bushes whose fruit turns gradually from pale green to pink to frosty blue. The ladies know they will have to fight the birds—and the bugs, and the bees—for every last berry, but effort is worth it.

Bridget freezes as many berries as she can for use later in the year in muffins and scones.

Ida Mae's Blueberry Scones

Ida Mae says . . . Everybody knows scones ain't nothing but biscuits with fruit baked in. Nobody but foreigners makes them in triangles.

- 1 cup flour
- ⅓ cup sugar
- ½ teaspoon salt
- ¼ teaspoon soda
- 1 egg
- ¼ cup buttermilk
- 2 tablespoons butter
- 1 cup blueberries

Preheat oven to 425.

Sift dry ingredients together. Chop the butter into small pieces and mix into the dry ingredients with your fingers or with a pastry cutter until the mixture forms fine crumbs.

Beat the egg. Add buttermilk to the egg mixture and beat to mix.

Mix the wet ingredients into the dry with your hands or with a spoon.

Stir in 1 cup blueberries, crushing a few with the back of the spoon to release the juices.

Generously butter an 8-inch baking sheet. Ida Mae uses a black iron skillet for hers, but any baking pan will do. Drop mixture by large spoonfuls onto the pan and bake at 425 for 18-20 minutes, until tops are golden brown. About 3 minutes before the scones are done, brush the tops with buttermilk and sprinkle with 2 tablespoons of sugar for a nice glaze.

Bridget's Elegant Blueberry Scones

Bridget says . . . This makes a very dense, more cake-like scone. The bright taste of lemon zest is what gives this recipe its zing.

- 1½ cups flour
- ½ cup sugar
- ¼ teaspoon salt
- 1½ teaspoons baking powder
- ¼ cup butter
- 1 egg
- ½ cup milk
- Zest of one lemon, very finely grated
- 1 cup blueberries

Preheat oven to 400.

Stir together first 4 ingredients. Cut in butter. Add milk and mix until smooth. Toss the blueberries with flour to coat (this keeps them from sinking to the bottom of the pan). Add blueberries to batter. Stir in grated lemon zest.

Generously butter an 8-inch cake pan or scone pan. Pour in the batter. Bake at 400 20-25 minutes, until golden on top and a wooden pick inserted in the center comes out clean. Cut into narrow wedges and serve hot with butter or lemon curd.

Blueberry Muffins

- 1 cup sugar
- ½ cup butter, softened
- 2 eggs
- ½ teaspoon vanilla extract
- 2 teaspoons baking powder
- 2¼ cups flour, divided
- ½ teaspoon salt
- 1½ cups blueberries

Preheat oven to 375. Butter 18 muffin cups or use paper liners.

Beat butter, sugar, eggs and vanilla together until smooth. Add baking powder, 2 cups of the flour, and the salt. Beat until smooth.

Toss blueberries with ¼ cup flour. Discard excess flour and gently stir blueberries into batter.

Fill muffin cups ⅔ full. Bake at 375 20-25 minutes.

Bridget says . . . Most people use oil in their muffin recipes. It's the butter that makes these muffins so irresistible!

Tomato Season

As every gardener knows, there's nothing better than the taste of a fresh tomato, still warm from the vine. You wait all season for the tomatoes to ripen, but when they do, they're all ready at once!

After you've eaten your fill and given away all the tomatoes your neighbors will take, what do you do with the remaining bushels? Here are a few ideas from the ladies of Ladybug Farm.

Tomato Basil Soup

- 1 clove garlic
- 2 tablespoons olive oil
- 6 cups roma tomatoes, peeled, seeded, and cut up
- ½ cup lightly packed fresh basil
- 1 tablespoon sugar
- ¼ teaspoon salt
- 1 cup beef broth
- Dash red pepper

Sauté garlic in olive oil until tender. Add remaining ingredients. Bring to boiling, then reduce heat. Cover and simmer for 30 minutes. Transfer to blender (working in small batches) and process until smooth. Garnish with fresh basil. May be served hot or cold.

Tomato Soup with Caramelized Onions

- 3 large onions, peeled and sliced
- 1 stick butter
- 10-12 large garden tomatoes, peeled and chopped
- 2 tablespoons sugar
- 3 cups beef broth
- 1 cup red wine
- Salt to taste

Melt butter in a large, heavy pan over medium heat. Add onions. Cook, stirring frequently, until onions are wilted and caramel in color, about 30 minutes.

In a large stock pot add tomatoes, broth, and caramelized onions. Cover and simmer over low heat approximately one hour. Add sugar and wine and continue to cook half an hour more. Taste and add salt if necessary.

Use an immersion blender to break up onions and tomatoes, but do not puree.

Serve hot, or freeze in quart containers for a winter's day.

Ida Mae says . . . The easiest way to peel tomatoes is to drop them into a pot of boiling water until the skins crack. Immediately place them in ice water until cool enough to handle. The skins slide right off!

Fresh Tomato Soup

- 4 cups peeled, chopped fresh tomatoes
- 1 sliced onion
- 2 cups chicken broth
- 2 tablespoons butter
- 2 tablespoons all-purpose flour
- 1 teaspoon salt
- 2 teaspoons sugar

Sauté onion in 2 tablespoons butter until tender. Add flour and stir quickly until thickened. Add chicken broth, a little at a time, stirring to avoid lumps. Add tomatoes, salt and sugar and simmer, covered, for 30 minutes. Transfer to a blender and blend until smooth.

Cream of Tomato Soup

- 6 large garden tomatoes, peeled and chopped
- 1 small onion, diced
- ½ stick butter
- 1½ cups chicken broth
- ½ cup heavy cream
- ½ teaspoon salt, or to taste

In a heavy 4-quart saucepan, sauté onion in butter until translucent. Add chicken broth, tomatoes and salt. Simmer, covered, 30 minutes.

Transfer soup to a blender in batches, or use an immersion blender, and blend until smooth. Return to pan and stir in cream. Cook to warm, but do not boil.

Serve warm or cold with a dollop of sour cream and crusty croutons.

Tomato Okra Soup

- 2 tablespoons butter
- 1 small onion, diced
- 1 small clove garlic, minced
- 1 rib celery, sliced
- 2 cups chicken broth
- 4 large tomatoes, peeled and roughly chopped
- 4 cups sliced fresh okra
- 1 cup cooked (or canned) corn
- 1 teaspoon Cajun seasoning
- Dash freshly ground black pepper
- Salt, to taste

In a medium saucepan, melt butter over medium-low heat. Add onion, garlic, and celery; cook and stir until celery is tender. Add chicken broth, tomatoes, sliced okra, corn, Cajun seasoning, and pepper. Bring to a boil. Reduce heat to medium-low, cover, and simmer for 30 minutes, or until okra is tender. Add salt to taste.

Tomato Chowder

- 4 bacon strips, cooked and crumbled
- ¼ cup butter or margarine
- ¼ cup all-purpose flour
- 2 cups chicken broth
- 2 fresh tomatoes, peeled and diced
- ⅔ cup half-and-half cream

Melt butter in a medium saucepan. Stir in flour until smooth. Gradually whisk in broth. Bring to a boil; cook and stir for 2 minutes or until thickened. Stir in tomatoes; heat through. Reduce heat; stir in cream. Heat through (do not boil). Stir in bacon and serve.

Bridget says . . . Make sure you cook your bacon fresh for this recipe. Don't use packaged pre-cooked bacon.

Company's Coming

Nothing is more exciting for the ladies of Ladybug Farm than having company. Whether they are entertaining overnight guests, or a group of friends for lunch, the floors are polished, the windows are gleaming, the linens are starched and the table is set with all their best. Ida Mae has even been known to iron the dishtowels!

Bridget brings out her richest desserts, Ida Mae makes sticky buns, and there's always plenty of breakfast casserole. As the day draws to a close, guests are invited to pull up a chair on the porch, pour a glass of wine, and enjoy one of the Shenandoah Valley's spectacular sunsets. Because one thing is certain: when you come visiting at Ladybug Farm, you're family.

Breakfast Casserole

- 6 slices day-old bread
- 1 pound mild sausage, cooked and drained
- 2 cups shredded cheddar cheese
- 6 eggs, beaten
- 2 cups milk
- 1 teaspoon dry mustard
- ½ teaspoon salt

Preheat oven to 350.

Grease the bottom of a 9x13 pan. Tear bread into 1-inch chunks. Sprinkle cooked crumbled sausage over bread pieces. Sprinkle cheddar cheese over the sausage. Mix eggs, milk, salt and mustard together; pour over casserole. Bake at 350 for 35 to 40 minutes.

Serves 4 to 6.

Bridget's Amaretto Peach Cobbler

- 6 fresh sweet peaches, peeled and sliced
- ¼ cup sugar
- 2 tablespoons amaretto

For topping:
- 1 stick very soft butter
- 1 cup sugar
- 1 cup flour
- 1 tablespoon amaretto
- ¼ teaspoon salt
- ¼ cup milk

Preheat oven to 400.

Butter an 8- or 9-inch oven-proof glass casserole dish.

Toss the peaches with ¼ cup sugar and 2 tablespoons amaretto and set aside.

Mix butter, sugar, flour, 1 tablespoon amaretto, salt, and milk until smooth.

Pour peach mixture into buttered casserole dish.

Top with batter. Bake at 400 for 20-30 minutes until golden and bubbly.

Serve warm with vanilla ice cream.

Beaten Biscuits

- 2 cups flour
- ¼ teaspoon salt
- ¼ teaspoon baking powder
- 2 tablespoons sugar
- ¼ cup chilled butter cut into small pieces
- ⅓ cup light cream
- Water, if needed

Preheat oven to 450.

Sift flour, salt, baking powder and sugar together.

Cut in the butter with your hands or a pastry cutter until mixture looks like coarse meal.

Use a standing mixer on low to mix dough. Add cream slowly until dough forms a ball. Add water if too dry.

Turn out onto a marble slab or floured wooden board and knead slightly.

With a mallet beat the dough into a rectangle.

Fold dough over then beat it out again.

Repeat this process until the dough becomes white and blisters form (about 15 minutes).

Roll out dough to ¼" thick.

Cut into 2-inch rounds and prick top with the tines of a fork.

Place on greased baking sheets and bake for 15 minutes.

Bridget says . . . Now that we have therapists to help deal with our frustrations, no one makes beaten biscuits anymore. But at least you don't have to worry about the calories—you use them all making the biscuits!

A Formal Luncheon

They were ready.

Four glasses of chilled peanut soup were lined up on the top shelf of the refrigerator. Maryland crab cakes and honey-glazed fried chicken were ready to be dropped into separate pans for frying, with the dill caper butter softening near the stove. The mini-quiches and caramelized onion tarts were baking, and the brie en croute was ready to be popped into the second oven. The midori sauce just needed to be heated. A bowl of chopped fresh heritage tomatoes, perfectly seasoned with herbs that had been cut from the garden only that morning, was ready to be spread on crisp garlic-infused baguette slices and topped with goat cheese. And, even though it was not part of the menu, Bridget had made a double fudge cake to be served with her special caramel sauce and fresh lavender whipped cream.

The porch was decorated with four round tables covered in multicolored calico topped with Battenberg lace. All four tables displayed center-pieces of roses fresh from their garden in various heirloom containers—a silver teapot, a china bowl, a coffee urn—and set with an eclectic mix of Limoges and Havilland. White Irish linen napkins trimmed with hand tatting were rolled inside twig napkin rings, each one accented with a rose bud. Even though it was two o'clock in the afternoon, candles flickered in crystal water glasses, and the flames were reflected in the cut glass wine glasses at each place setting. Only one table had chairs around it, and on that table was a tray of four sparkling mimosas in champagne flutes.

Lindsay and Bridget looked cool and collected in light summer dresses, with their hair swept back and their makeup touched up at least twice in the past hour. Rebel was in the barn with a padlock on the door. The gate to the chicken yard, likewise, was latched and locked. The goat and the deer were in separate stalls inside the barn. And the smell of fertilizer was, for the most part, but a distant memory. They were ready.

—Love Letters from Ladybug Farm

Peanut Soup

- 2 cups chicken stock
- 2 tablespoons chopped onion
- 1 tablespoon butter
- ½ cup peanut butter
- ½ cup milk
- Chopped peanuts for garnish

Sauté the onions in butter until tender. Add chicken stock and simmer for 10-20 minutes. Add peanut butter and stir until melted. Do not boil. Transfer mixture to blender (or use an immersion blender) and process until blended. Return to heat and add milk. Simmer until warmed through, but do not boil.

May be served hot, or delicious cold, served in martini glasses with cheese straws. Garnish with chopped peanuts before serving.

Honey-Glazed Fried Chicken

- 2 pounds boneless skinless chicken breasts, cut into 2-inch pieces
- 1 egg, beaten
- ¼ cup milk
- ½ cup flour
- ½ teaspoon salt
- ⅛ teaspoon pepper
- Vegetable oil for frying

For glaze:
- ⅓ cup butter
- ⅓ cup honey
- 1 teaspoon cinnamon
- ½ cup finely ground pecans

Mix together flour, salt and pepper. In a separate bowl, beat eggs and milk until combined. Dip chicken pieces in egg mixture, then in flour mixture. Heat ½-inch oil in a large frying pan over medium-high heat and add chicken in batches. Do not overcrowd. Cook until chicken golden brown, turning as needed. Drain on paper towels, and keep warm while preparing the glaze.

Melt butter in a small saucepan and add honey and cinnamon, stirring until honey is melted. Immediately dip pieces of warm chicken in the glaze and roll in crushed pecans.

Mini-Quiches

- 1 cup grated cheddar
- 3 tablespoons flour
- 3 eggs, beaten
- ⅔ cup mayonnaise
- 1 cup broccoli, fresh or frozen, chopped very fine
- 8 slices bacon, cooked, crumbled
- ½ cup fresh mushrooms, chopped
- ½ teaspoon salt
- Dash of freshly ground pepper

Preheat oven to 350. Grease 24 mini muffin cups.

In a medium bowl stir flour into cheese. Add remaining ingredients; mix well. Fill muffin cups with mixture. Bake at 350 for 20 minutes or until set. Let cool slightly before removing from tins.

Caramelized Onion Tart

- 6 medium sized sweet onions, like Vidalia, sliced
- 1 stick butter
- 3 eggs
- ½ cup heavy cream
- ¼ teaspoon nutmeg
- 1 teaspoon salt
- 3 slices Swiss cheese
- 1 tablespoon prepared Dijon mustard
- 1 9-inch pie crust

Preheat oven to 350.

Melt butter in a large, heavy skillet. Add onions and cook over medium heat, stirring occasionally, until onions are soft and browned, forming a thick caramel colored sauce.

Beat together eggs, cream, nutmeg, and salt.

Brush the bottom of the pie crust with mustard. Place caramelized onions in the crust and top with cheese. Pour the egg mixture on top.

Bake at 350 for 30-35 minutes, until top is golden brown.

Wedding Dinner Menu

Appetizer:

Three berry fruit cup in balsamic vinaigrette
topped with gorgonzola crumbles and
toasted black walnuts, served with
miniature cheese biscuits

Soup:

Chilled cantaloupe soup
with mint and crème fraiche

Entree:

Free range roast turkey wrapped in
applewood smoked bacon served on a
bed of fresh cherry conserve and accompanied
by fingerling potatoes and baby carrots
sautéed in rosemary-infused olive oil

Summer squash soufflé

Garden fresh green beans, lightly sautéed
and tossed with thyme, toasted almonds
and baby onions

Dessert:

Strawberry crumble topped with
homemade vanilla ice cream

—Love Letters From Ladybug Farm

Three Berry Fruit Cup

- ½ cup extra-virgin olive oil
- ½ cup white balsamic vinegar
- 1 clove crushed garlic
- 2 tablespoons fresh minced thyme
- 1 tablespoon fresh chopped mint
- 1 pinch salt
- Ground black pepper to taste
- 1 cup blackberries
- 1 cup blueberries
- 1 cup raspberries
- Gorgonzola cheese for garnish
- ½ cup black walnuts, chopped and toasted, for garnish

In a small bowl, whisk together olive oil, white balsamic vinegar, garlic, thyme and mint. Season to taste with salt and black pepper.

Combine berries in a large bowl. Toss lightly with vinaigrette.

Serve in individual bowls or glasses. Top each with one tablespoon crumbled gorgonzola cheese and one tablespoon toasted black walnuts.

Chilled Cantaloupe Soup
with Mint and Crème Fraiche

- 1 cantaloupe, peeled, seeded, and cubed
- 2 cups orange juice
- 1 tablespoon fresh lemon juice
- ¼ cup fresh mint

Peel, seed, and cube the cantaloupe.

Place cantaloupe, ½ cup orange juice and mint in a blender or food processor; cover, and process until smooth. Transfer to large bowl. Stir in lemon juice and remaining orange juice. Cover, and refrigerate for at least one hour. Garnish with mint and crème fraiche (recipe follows).

Crème Fraiche

- 1 cup heavy whipping cream
- 1 tablespoon buttermilk

In a medium saucepan over low heat, warm the cream to 105 degrees F. Remove from heat and stir in the buttermilk. Transfer the cream to a large bowl and allow this mixture to stand in a warm place, loosely covered with plastic wrap, until thickened but still of pouring consistency. Stir and taste every 6-8 hours. This process takes anywhere from 24 to 36 hours, depending on your room temperature. The crème fraiche is ready when it is thick with a slightly nutty sour taste. Chill cream, in the refrigerator, for several hours.

Roasted Turkey in Applewood Bacon

- 1 fresh, not frozen, free range turkey, approx. 15 pounds
- Juice of one lemon
- Salt and pepper
- ½ cup butter
- 1 yellow onion, peeled and quartered
- Tops and bottoms of a bunch of celery
- 2 carrots
- Parsley
- Sprigs of fresh rosemary
- 6-8 slices applewood-smoked bacon
- 2 cloves garlic, halved

24 hours in advance:

Brine the turkey overnight by placing it in a mixture of 1 cup salt to 1 gallon water (or water to cover) and refrigerate, covered, for 6-12 hours.

In the morning, remove the turkey from the brine and discard the brine. Wash the turkey with water and pat dry.

Preheat the oven to 400.

Lather the inside of the cavity with the juice of half a lemon. Take a small handful of salt and rub all over the inside of the turkey. Quarter the lemon and place inside the cavity of the turkey.

Add the onion, peeled and quartered, a bunch of parsley, a couple of carrots, and some tops and bottoms of celery.

Make small slits beneath the skin and insert the quartered garlic and sprigs of rosemary. Wrap the turkey in applewood-smoked bacon and secure with metal skewers. Make sure that the turkey's legs are tied together, held close to the body, and tie a string around the turkey body to hold the wings in close.

Place turkey BREAST DOWN on the bottom of a rack over a sturdy roasting pan big enough to catch all the drippings.

Cook at **400** for the **first half an hour**. Then reduce the heat to **350** for the **next 2 hours**. Then reduce the heat further to **225** for the **next hour to hour and a half**.

Turn the turkey over for **the last 15 minutes** of cooking, at an oven temp of **300**, to brown the breast.

Turkey is done when a meat thermometer inserted into the thigh reads **175**. Let turkey rest out of the oven for 15-20 minutes, and carve breast side up.

Serve on a bed of cherry conserve (recipe follows).

Cherry Conserve

- 2 pounds sweet cherries, pitted
- 1 orange
- 4 cups sugar
- Juice of ½ lemon
- 1 cup seedless raisins
- 1 cup chopped pecans

Chop the cherries coarsely.

Seed the orange and slice very thin.

Mix the cherries, sliced orange, sugar, and lemon juice in a large pan; cook slowly, stirring, until the mixture is thick and transparent. Add the raisins and nuts and continue cooking 5 minutes.

Summer Squash Soufflé

- 2 pounds sliced yellow summer squash
- 1 medium onion, chopped
- 1 teaspoon salt
- 1 cup milk
- 2 eggs, lightly beaten
- 3 tablespoons melted butter
- 3 tablespoons flour
- 1 cup shredded cheddar cheese
- Seasoned salt and pepper, to taste
- Buttered bread crumbs

Combine squash, onion, and salt in a large saucepan; cover with water and simmer until vegetables are tender, about 15 to 20 minutes. Drain and mash well. Stir in milk, eggs, melted butter, flour and cheese. Add salt and pepper to taste. Preheat oven to 350. Bake in a buttered 1½-quart casserole for about 30 minutes. Top with buttered bread crumbs and bake for about 10 minutes longer.

Bridget says . . . Technically, this is more of a casserole than a soufflé, but it's so light and airy no one minds if I call it a soufflé!

Strawberry Crumble

- 2 cups sliced strawberries
- ½ cup sugar
- 2 cups flour
- 4 teaspoons baking powder
- 1 cup sugar
- 1 teaspoon salt
- ½ cup butter
- ⅔ cup milk
- 1 egg, slightly beaten

For topping:
- ¼ cup butter
- ¼ cup sugar
- ½ cup flour

Cover strawberries with ½ cup sugar and set aside. Sift flour, baking powder, 1 cup sugar, and salt. Cut in butter. Combine milk with egg and stir into flour mixture, blending well. Pour strawberry-sugar mixture into well-buttered baking dish, top with batter. Mix together ¼ cup butter, ¼ cup sugar and ½ cup flour with a fork. Sprinkle over mixture in baking pan. Bake at 350 until bubbly and golden brown, 20-30 minutes. Serve with homemade vanilla ice cream (recipe follows).

Homemade Vanilla Ice Cream

- 4 egg yolks
- ½ pint whole milk
- ½ pint heavy cream
- 1 cup sugar
- 1 vanilla pod (scored down the middle)
- 1 tablespoon vanilla extract

Pour the milk into a saucepan and bring slowly up to boiling point but do not boil. Remove from heat and place the vanilla pod into the mixture. Leave to infuse for about 20 minutes.

In a bowl, beat and mix together the egg yolks and sugar until thick. Carefully remove the vanilla pod from the pan of milk and scrape out the seeds into the milk. Pour the milk into the mixture of egg yolks and sugar while stirring. Pour the mixture back into the pan and heat gently, stirring until the custard thickens, but do not boil. Remove from heat and stir in vanilla extract. Cool in refrigerator 6 hours or overnight. Stir the cream into the cold custard base and transfer the whole mixture into an ice cream maker. Freeze according to manufacturer's directions.

Autumn

Harvest Time

They made zucchini bread, zucchini casserole, fried, sautéed and roasted zucchini. They made squash soup, tomato soup, onion soup and enough marinara sauce to open an Italian restaurant. They chopped pears for chutney and simmered them into a sweet thick sauce and ate them whole, with juices dripping down their wrists and chins, over the sink. Everything else was put on hold for a season that wouldn't wait, and the abundance of nature's harvest took over their lives.

They bought a second freezer and installed it in the cellar. They shaved corn off the cob and packed it into plastic pint containers, blanched green beans, lima beans, okra and field peas and did the same. And of course they couldn't ignore the bounty of their own fruit trees and bushes when they began to produce. Bridget added twenty-seven glistening jars of blackberry jam to the raspberry coulis in the pantry, and at least as many jars of cherry jelly, grape jelly and apple sauce. They wondered out loud just how long gardens could possibly continue to produce in this region, anyway.

—A Year on Ladybug Farm

Zucchini Casserole

- 3 large, unpeeled zucchini, sliced
- ¼ cup chopped onion
- 1 (10.75 ounce) can condensed cream of chicken soup
- 2 cups shredded cheddar cheese
- 1 cup sour cream
- 1 stick unsalted butter, melted
- 3 cups dry bread crumbs
- ½ teaspoon salt
- ¼ teaspoon black pepper

Preheat oven to 350.

Butter a 9x13-inch baking dish.

Boil the zucchini and onion in water for 5 minutes; drain well. In a medium bowl, combine the soup, sour cream and cheese. Stir in the zucchini and onion and mix well.

In a separate medium bowl, combine the butter, bread crumbs, salt and pepper. Spread half of this mixture into the bottom of a 9x13-inch baking dish. Spoon the zucchini mixture over the bread crumbs, then top off with the other half of the bread crumb mixture.

Bake at 350 for 25 to 30 minutes, or until golden brown.

Zucchini Bread

- 3 eggs
- 1 cup vegetable oil
- 1¾ cups sugar
- 2 cups grated zucchini
- 1 teaspoon vanilla
- 3 cups flour
- ½ teaspoon salt
- ½ teaspoon baking powder
- 1 teaspoon baking soda
- 1 teaspoon nutmeg
- 1 tablespoon cinnamon
- ½ cup pecans

Preheat oven to 350. Grease and flour 2 loaf pans.

Mix together eggs, oil, sugar, zucchini, and vanilla with electric mixer until smooth. Add remaining ingredients and mix until well combined.

Pour into 2 greased and floured loaf pans. Bake at 350 for approximately 45 to 50 minutes or until the center springs back when touched.

Butternut Squash Soup

- 1 medium (3 pound) butternut squash
- 2 tablespoons butter
- 2 tablespoons brown sugar
- 1 teaspoon nutmeg
- 1 medium onion, halved
- 6 cups chicken stock
- Salt and freshly ground black pepper
- ½ cup heavy cream
- Sour cream for garnish

Preheat oven to 400.

Cut squash in half and scoop out seeds and stringy flesh. Place squash, cut side up, on an oiled baking sheet. Fill the hollow of each half of the squash with 1 tablespoon butter, 1 tablespoon brown sugar, and ½ teaspoon nutmeg. Top with halved onion.

Roast squash and onion mixture 30-45 minutes until squash is very soft. Remove from oven and set aside until cool enough to handle.

Scoop all of the squash flesh and the onion into a saucepan. Be sure to include any juices or spices that remain on the baking sheet. Add chicken stock and simmer 30 minutes to blend flavors. Transfer to a blender and blend until smooth. Return to saucepan, add salt and pepper to taste, and stir in cream. Heat through. Serve warm with a dollop of sour cream.

Harvest Marinara Sauce

- 12 medium ripe tomatoes, peeled and chopped
- 2 large onions, peeled and diced
- 6 cloves garlic, peeled and minced
- ¼ cup olive oil
- 1 green bell pepper, chopped
- 2 carrots, chopped
- ¼ cup fresh basil, chopped
- ¼ cup fresh oregano, chopped
- ¼ cup fresh marjoram or thyme, chopped
- 1 cup Burgundy wine
- 1 bay leaf
- 2 stalks celery
- 2 tablespoons tomato paste
- 2 tablespoons beef bouillon granules

In a large soup pot, heat olive oil on medium heat. Add onions and cook until caramelized. Add the garlic and fresh herbs and cook for 5 minutes. Do not allow garlic to brown. Add remaining ingredients and cook on low, covered, stirring occasionally for about 2 hours. Working in batches, transfer all but 1 cup of the sauce to a blender and blend until smooth. Add 1 cup of unprocessed sauce for texture, and stir to mix well. Salt and pepper to taste.

Miss Emily's
Cook Book

"I love Brunswick stew." Cici leaned in to peer at the recipe. "Tomatoes, butterbeans, onions, corn . . . this is perfect! We can use all these vegetables in one big stew!"

Bridget wrinkled her nose and she dragged her finger down the list of ingredients. "Venison . . ."

"Use beef," suggested Cici.

"Duck . . ."

"Chicken."

"Hog jowls?"

"Pork loin."

"It says here to slow roast the meat on a spit over an open fire."

Now it was Cici's turn to wrinkle her nose. "When was that thing written anyway? During the American Revolution?"

Bridget looked up from the book. "Wait. We've got Lindsay's propane grill stored in the barn. We haven't used it all summer."

"We've been too busy peeling vegetables."

"That's an open flame, isn't it?"

"It sure is," agreed Cici. "We can get rid of every last vegetable in this kitchen today!"

—A Year on Ladybug Farm

Miss Emily's Brunswick Stew
As interpreted by Cici

Rub for meats:
- 4 tablespoons paprika
- 4 tablespoons kosher salt
- ½ cup brown sugar
- 2 tablespoons freshly ground black pepper
- ½ tablespoon cayenne pepper
- 2 tablespoons onion powder
- 2 tablespoons garlic powder
- 2 tablespoons olive oil

Mix all ingredients together. Rub on meats.

- 3-4 pound boneless pork loin roast
- 4-5 pound boneless beef chuck roast
- 2-3 pounds skinless boneless chicken thighs and breasts

Prepare barbecue grill to medium-high heat. Add 1 cup hickory chips that have been soaked in water for 30 minutes and drained. Immediately place meats that have been prepared with barbecue rub on the grill and close the top of the grill to infuse with flavor. Watch for flame-ups as the fat content of the meat and the sugar in the rub will burn quickly. The object is to sear the meat, blacken the rub, and infuse with smoke. The meat does not have to be cooked through, although it is helpful if most of the fat is seared off.

Remove meats from grill when outer crust is brown or slightly charred. Let rest until cool enough to handle. Chop meats roughly, removing and discarding any fat.

In a large (5 gallon or larger) stew pot combine:

- 1 gallon peeled fresh tomatoes, chopped
- 2 quarts fresh corn
- 2 quarts shelled fresh butterbeans
- 1 quart sliced fresh okra (optional)
- ¼ cup Worcestershire sauce, or more to taste
- ½ cup apple cider vinegar

Add chopped meats to this mixture and bring to a boil. Reduce heat immediately and simmer for 2-3 hours, until all meats are cooked through and vegetables are soft. Taste broth and season if necessary.

Transfer in batches to a food processor, and grind until meats and vegetables are blended. Return all batches to the pot and cook for 20-30 minutes to blend flavors. Taste against for seasoning.

Freeze in quart containers to enjoy all winter!

Bridget's Apple Currant Pie

- ¼ cup bourbon
- 1 cup currants
- 1½ cups sugar
- 1½ cups flour
- 1 teaspoon cinnamon
- ½ teaspoon nutmeg
- ¼ teaspoon salt
- ¼ teaspoon ground cloves
- 6 peeled and sliced Granny Smith apples
- ⅔ cup firmly packed brown sugar
- ½ cup butter
- 1 10-inch pie crust

In a small bowl, combine bourbon and currants. Cover and let stand overnight.

Preheat oven to 375.

Prepare a 10-inch pie crust, or a 9-inch deep dish crust.

In a large bowl, mix 1½ cups granulated sugar, ½ cup flour, spices, and salt.

Remove currants from bourbon with a slotted spoon; reserve bourbon. Add currants and apples to sugar mixture and mix well.

Pour filling into unbaked 10-inch pie pastry in pan. Drizzle evenly with reserved bourbon.

In another bowl, mix 1 cup flour and the brown sugar.

Add butter and cut in with a pastry blender or rub with your fingers until mixture forms small lumps.

Sprinkle topping evenly over filling.

Set pie on a baking pan and bake at 375 for 55 to 65 minutes. Cover loosely with foil if pie crust browns too quickly.

Pie is done when apples are tender and juices bubble to the top.

Winter

Comfort Food

There's something about a cold north wind, night that comes too early, and a fire crackling in the fireplace that makes everyone crave creamy, fatty, high-carb dishes . . . otherwise known as comfort food.

Comfort food is a specialty of mothers everywhere, whether it be served at the kitchen table or wrapped in a care package to a college student or a soldier overseas. As Lori says in *Love Letters from Ladybug Farm*:

Can you e-mail me some mac and cheese?:)

Three-Cheese Macaroni

- 2 cups cooked pasta—penne, angel hair, elbow macaroni, or a mixture of your favorites
- 2 tablespoons butter
- ¼ cup flour
- Salt and pepper to taste
- ¼ teaspoon nutmeg
- 1 cup milk
- ¼ cup shredded asiago cheese
- ¼ cup sharp white cheddar, grated
- ¼ cup shredded Swiss cheese
- 2 cups grated yellow cheddar
- ⅓ cup dry bread crumbs
- 2 tablespoons butter

Melt butter in a 2 quart saucepan. Add flour, salt, pepper and nutmeg. Stirring continuously, slowly add milk. Add asiago, sharp white cheddar, and Swiss cheeses and cook and stir over low heat until cheeses are melted and mixture starts to thicken. Remove from heat.

In a small buttered casserole dish layer half the pasta. Sprinkle with 1 cup grated yellow cheddar. Pour half the cheese sauce over this. Top with remaining pasta, remaining cheese sauce, and a mixture of 1 cup cheddar and ⅓ cup bread crumbs. Dot with butter.

Bake at 350 until bubbly and golden brown, approximately 20 minutes.

Ida Mae says . . . There's nothing like a good bowl of hearty vegetable soup and a wedge of buttered cornbread to take the chill out of your bones.

Bridget says . . . Or my beef stew.

Buttermilk Cornbread

- 1 cup cornmeal
- ⅓ cup all-purpose flour
- ¼ teaspoon baking soda
- 1 teaspoon baking powder
- 1 teaspoon salt
- 1 egg, beaten
- 1 cup buttermilk

Heat oven to 400. Slather a 9-inch iron skillet with grease and place inside the oven to heat.

Combine dry ingredients; add beaten egg and buttermilk, mixing well. Pour into greased, heated 9-inch iron skillet. Batter should sizzle and puff up around the edges when it hits the skillet.

Bake at 400 for 20 minutes, or until lightly browned.

Ida Mae's Homemade Vegetable Soup

- 1 medium onion, chopped
- 2 tablespoons olive oil
- 1 quart (32 ounces) peeled, chopped tomatoes with juice
- 1 quart (32 ounces) butterbeans
- 2 cups corn
- 2 cups peeled, chopped potatoes
- 3 quarts beef stock
- Salt to taste
- ⅓ cup fresh chopped mixed herbs—rosemary, thyme, marjoram, basil or oregano work well

In a large stock pan sauté chopped onion in olive oil until tender. Add remaining ingredients, cover, and simmer on low heat 1-2 hours, until vegetables are tender and flavors are blended. Taste and adjust salt if needed.

Note: If freezing, omit potatoes. Cooked potatoes can be added to thawed and reheated soup just before serving, if desired.

Bridget's Beef Stew

- ¼ cup extra-virgin olive oil
- 3 tablespoons butter
- 2 cups all-purpose flour
- 2 to 3 pounds cubed beef stew meat
- Sea salt and freshly ground black pepper
- 1 cup Burgundy wine
- 8 fresh thyme sprigs
- 3 garlic cloves, smashed
- 2 bay leaves
- 3 cups beef stock
- 9 small new potatoes, scrubbed clean and cut in half
- 6 carrots, peeled and sliced
- 2 small onions, quartered
- 1 cup garden peas, frozen or fresh
- 4 large tomatoes, peeled and quartered, or 2 (16-ounce cans) tomatoes with juice

Preheat a large heavy-bottomed saucepan or Dutch oven over medium-high heat and melt the oil and butter.

Season the beef with salt and pepper, dredge in flour, and brown all of the cubes in the hot oil mixture on all sides. Add remaining ingredients; cover and cook on low heat for 2½ hours.

Chicken with
Cracked Cranberry Dressing

- 6-pound hen

For dressing:
- 1 stick butter
- 1 cup finely chopped celery
- 1 medium onion, minced
- ½ cup fresh or frozen cranberries
- 4 squares cornbread, crumbled
- 4 slices toast, diced
- 1 teaspoon poultry seasoning
- 1 egg
- ½ teaspoon salt
- ¼ teaspoon pepper
- ¾ cup chicken broth

- 2 tablespoons butter for hen

Sauté celery, onion and cranberries in butter until onion is translucent and cranberries are cracked. Mix cornbread and toast with poultry seasoning, salt, pepper and egg. Add vegetable mixture and chicken broth. Mix so all ingredients are moist. Rub hen with one tablespoon butter. Cut remaining tablespoon into small pieces and insert under skin. Stuff the dressing loosely into the neck and body cavities. Roast 2½-3 hours at 325. Left-over dressing may be baked separately for the last 45 minutes of roasting.

Roast Pork Loin

- 3 cloves garlic, minced
- 3 tablespoons fresh rosemary, plus
  10-12 sprigs to line the serving platter
- Salt and pepper to taste
- 2 pounds boneless pork loin roast
- ¼ cup olive oil
- ½ cup white wine

Preheat oven to 350.

Crush garlic with rosemary, salt and pepper, making a paste. Pierce meat with a sharp knife in several places and press the garlic paste into the openings. Rub the meat with the remaining garlic mixture and 1 tablespoon olive oil.

Mix remaining olive oil and wine. Place pork loin in pan and pour the olive oil mixture over it. Cook, turning frequently to baste with pan liquids, until pork is no longer pink in the center, about 2 hours. An instant-read thermometer inserted into the center should read 160 degrees F. Remove roast to a platter lined with rosemary. Serve with pan juices.

Horseradish Mashed Potatoes

- 4 pounds golden creamer potatoes
- Kosher salt and freshly ground black pepper
- 2 cups sour cream
- 1 stick unsalted butter
- 3 tablespoons prepared horseradish
- 2 tablespoons cooking water
- Chopped fresh chives, for garnish

Put the potatoes into a large pot, add 2 tablespoons salt, and cover with cold water. Bring to a boil over medium-high heat and cook until the potatoes are tender, about 20 minutes. Drain the water from the potatoes, reserving 2 tablespoons cooking water. Smash potatoes in a large mixing bowl. Add the sour cream, butter, horseradish and season well with salt and pepper. Garnish with chopped fresh chives. Makes 6-8 servings.

Ida Mae's Bourbon Pecan Pie

- 6 tablespoons unsalted butter, softened
- 1 cup dark brown sugar
- 3 eggs
- 1 teaspoon vanilla extract
- ½ teaspoon salt
- ¾ cup dark corn syrup
- 3 tablespoons bourbon
- 2 cups pecan halves or pieces, divided
- 1 pie shell, 9-inch, unbaked

Beat together the butter and brown sugar until creamy and light. Add eggs, one at a time, beating after each addition. Beat in vanilla, salt, corn syrup, and bourbon. Arrange 1 cup pecans on the bottom of the pie shell. Pour pie filling over the pecans, then sprinkle remaining pecans over filling. Bake 55 to 60 minutes at 350.

Sticky Buns

- 1 teaspoon white sugar
- 1 package active dry yeast
- ½ cup lukewarm water
- ½ cup milk
- ¼ cup white sugar
- ¼ cup butter
- 1 teaspoon salt
- 2 eggs, beaten
- 4 cups all-purpose flour
- ¾ cup butter
- ¾ cup brown sugar
- 1 cup chopped pecans, divided
- ¾ cup brown sugar
- 1 tablespoon ground cinnamon
- ¼ cup melted butter

In a small bowl, dissolve 1 teaspoon sugar and yeast in warm water. Let stand until creamy, about 10 minutes. Warm the milk in a small saucepan until it bubbles, then remove from heat. Mix in ¼ cup sugar, ¼ cup butter and salt; stir until melted. Let cool until lukewarm.

In a large bowl, combine the yeast mixture, milk mixture, eggs and 1½ cups flour; stir well to combine. Stir in the remaining flour, ½ cup at a time, beating well after each addition. When the dough has pulled together, turn it out onto a lightly floured surface and knead until smooth and elastic, about 8 minutes.

Lightly butter a large bowl; place the dough in the bowl and turn to coat with butter. Cover with a damp cloth and let rise in a warm place until doubled in volume, about one hour.

While dough is rising, melt ¾ cup butter in a small saucepan over medium heat. Stir in ¾ cup brown sugar, whisking until smooth. Pour into greased 9x13-inch baking pan. Sprinkle bottom of pan with ½ cup pecans; set aside. Melt remaining butter; set aside. Combine remaining ¾ cup brown sugar, ½ cup pecans, and cinnamon; set aside.

Turn dough out onto a lightly floured surface, roll into an 18x14-inch rectangle. Brush with 2 tablespoons melted butter, leaving ½-inch border uncovered; sprinkle with brown sugar cinnamon mixture. Starting at long side, tightly roll up, pinching seam to seal. Brush with remaining 2 tablespoons butter. With serrated knife, cut into 15 pieces; place cut side down, in prepared pan. Cover and let rise for one hour or until doubled in volume. Meanwhile, preheat oven to 375 degrees.

Bake in preheated oven for 25 to 30 minutes, until golden brown. Let cool in pan for 3 minutes, then invert onto serving platter. Scrape remaining filling from the pan onto the rolls.

Bridget says . . . These are a lot of trouble, but nothing warms a house like the smell of cinnamon and yeast rolls in the morning.

Ida Mae says . . . Unless you're the one that's got to get out of bed at four a.m. to make them.

Ida Mae's Meat Loaf

- 2 pounds ground beef
- 1 egg
- 1 onion, chopped
- 2 tablespoons green pepper, chopped
- 1 tablespoon olive oil
- 1 cup milk
- 2 tablespoons Worcestershire sauce
- 1 cup dried bread crumbs
- Salt and pepper to taste
- 4 tablespoons brown sugar
- 2 tablespoons prepared mustard
- ⅔ cup ketchup
- ½ cup cheddar cheese

Preheat oven to 350.

Sauté onion and green pepper in olive oil until tender.

In a large bowl, combine the beef, egg, sautéed vegetables, milk and bread crumbs and Worcestershire. Season with salt and pepper to taste and place in a lightly greased 5x9-inch loaf pan.

In a separate small bowl, combine the brown sugar, mustard and ketchup. Mix well and pour over the meat loaf.

Bake at 350 for 45 minutes. Top with cheddar cheese. Continue cooking for 15 minutes longer.

Christmas

The annual Huntington Lane Christmas Party, jointly hosted by Cici, Lindsay and Bridget in Cici's home, was an event without parallel. Friends, neighbors, colleagues and families shopped all year for the perfect dress, the just-right shoes, the unprecedented hostess gifts. The ladies themselves held their first organizational meeting in September, and from Labor Day onward the clock was counting down toward what was to be, each and every year, the party that would leave all previous parties in the dust.

A graceful draped rope of tiny blue lights lined both sides of Cici's driveway from the street to the house. A miniature Christmas tree, decorated in twinkling blue and white lights, adorned the fish pond which was the centerpiece of her front lawn while overhead every branch of every deciduous tree was wrapped in tiny white lights and hung with oversized, interior-lit, blue glass ornaments. The front porch was swagged with greenery and studded with white lights and pink poinsettia leaves, and the double entry doors showcased twin wreaths in which glittery white lights and blue satin ribbon were woven in and out of bouquets of white roses.

The foyer was dominated by a fourteen foot,

snow white Christmas tree done completely in crystal ornaments and blue lights. Every doorway was swagged in fake-snow-frosted greenery that was interwoven with blue satin ribbon and tiny white lights. To the right of the tree was a bar, draped with white satin and decorated with sprays of white roses and a half dozen blue candles, where a bartender made certain every guest was immediately greeted with a cup of creamy Southern Comfort eggnog. Hidden stereo speakers provided traditional Christmas music as a background to the "Oohs" and "ahhs" and the happy greetings of guests who only saw one another once a year.

In the study, Cici's office furniture had been pushed against the wall and covered by floor-to-ceiling drapes of theatrical scrim which were backlit by red and green up-lights and draped with swags of evergreen tied with elaborate red bows and clusters of sparkly ornaments. In the center of the room was a twelve foot evergreen decorated in gold balls and red and green lights. Surrounding it, Cici had built a circular serving table that was draped in gold lamé and lit by dozens of gold candles on mirrors. Behind the table another bartender prepared pomegranate margaritas while guests plucked shrimp from the Christmas-tree shaped tower decorated with red pepper ornaments and filled their gold-colored hors d'oeuvres plates with everything from homemade cheese straws to olives wrapped in prosciutto.

The dining room buffet was an L-shaped spectacle of white satin, silver ornaments and red glass. Rows upon rows of glittering white lights were tucked into nests of greenery and draped through folds of satin, while red glass ball ornaments reflected the sparkle and clusters of red roses accented each serving dish. The Beef Wellington was a work of art with its crispy pastry crust and savory spinach filling, complemented by an asparagus casserole for which Bridget would never reveal the recipe. The flaky rolls had been three days in the making. Mushrooms had been stuffed and frozen a week in advance. Crispy crab cakes on a heated platter surrounded a silver bowl of remoulade sauce. New potatoes had been tossed with a hot tomato vinaigrette mere moments before serving, and were kept warm with a chafing dish. Vegetarian selections included a broccoli quiche, tomato tarts with black olives, and a six layer cheese, red pepper, and pesto torte. The desert buffet featured a Christmas tree decorated with sugared fruit and surrounded by a colorful wreath of decorated cookies—all lovingly handmade of course— bowls of truffles and dipping chocolate, three different layer cakes, and the piece de resistance —individual custard cups, trimmed in silver paper and filled with peppermint cream.

—A Year on Ladybug Farm

Derrick's Asparagus Puffs

- 24 fresh asparagus tips
- 14-ounce puff pastry sheet
- 1 wheel of brie
- 24 thin strips of prosciutto
- Honey mustard

Preheat oven to 400.

Blanch asparagus tips just until tender, about 3 minutes. Pat dry with paper towels.

Roll out the puff pastry and cut into 24 slices. Spread each slice with honey mustard. Place a strip of prosciutto on each one, followed by a ¼-inch thick slice of brie. Press an asparagus tip into the cheese on each pastry strip, and roll the pastry up to cover the asparagus, sealing the ends. Make sure the cheese is completely covered.

Bake at 400 until pastry is puffed and golden, 10 to 12 minutes.

Bite Sized Zucchini Tarts

- 10x13-inch sheet of frozen puff pastry, thawed and chilled
- 12 small zucchini (about 2½ pounds), trimmed
- Salt
- 3 tablespoons butter
- 1 small onion, finely chopped
- 10 cherry tomatoes, excess moisture pressed out, finely chopped
- 1 cup crumbled feta cheese
- ½ cup ricotta
- 2 tablespoons chopped fresh basil
- Freshly ground black pepper
- 1 egg, lightly beaten

Preheat oven to 350.

Cut rounds of puff pastry to fit 24 well-greased mini muffin tins. Place pastry in tin and bake about 25 minutes, until golden. Cool.

Grate 4 zucchini into a large bowl. Add 1 tablespoon of salt, toss well, and set aside to let weep for 30 minutes. Transfer to a stack of paper towels and press thoroughly to remove moisture.

Meanwhile, slice remaining zucchini into ¼-inch thick rounds. Blanch in a large pot of boiling salted water for one minute. Drain and spread out on paper towels.

Heat butter in a large skillet over medium heat. Add onions and cook until soft, 5-6 minutes. Add grated zucchini and cook, stirring often, until just beginning to brown, 5-7 minutes. Transfer to a large bowl; let cool.

Stir tomatoes, egg, half of the feta, ricotta, basil, and salt and pepper to taste into zucchini mixture. Spread mixture evenly in individual crusts. Arrange zucchini rounds, slightly overlapping in rows, like tiles, on top. Bake for 15 minutes, then brush top with reserved butter. Continue to bake until crust is deep golden, 10 minutes more. Let cool to room temperature, then sprinkle remaining feta over top.

Ida Mae's Yeast Rolls

- 2 tablespoons butter, softened
- 3 tablespoons white sugar
- 1 cup hot water
- 1 (.25 ounce) package active dry yeast
- 1 egg, beaten
- 1 teaspoon salt
- 2¼ cups all-purpose flour
- 1 tablespoon melted butter (for brushing tops of rolls)

Preheat oven to 425.

In a large bowl, mix the butter, sugar, and hot water. Allow to cool until lukewarm, and mix in the yeast until dissolved. Mix in the egg, salt, and flour. Allow the dough to rise until doubled in size.

Form dough into rolls with your floured hands by pinching off a 2-inch section and forming it into a ball. Place rolls on a greased baking sheet, and allow to rise again until doubled in size.

Brush tops of rolls with 1 tablespoon melted butter. Bake for 10 minutes in the preheated oven, or until a knife inserted in the center of a roll comes out clean.

Serve hot with butter and honey.

Beef Wellington

- 6 (4- to 5-ounce) tenderloin steaks
- ½ teaspoon salt
- ¼ teaspoon pepper
- ½ cup chopped onion
- ⅓ cup vegetable oil
- 1 cup red wine
- 2 tablespoons brandy
- ½ teaspoon fines herbes
- 1 tablespoon butter or margarine, melted
- Spinach Stuffing (recipe follows)
- Prepared pastry or filo dough (from the refrigerated section of your grocer)
- 2 egg yolks
- 2 teaspoons water

Sprinkle steaks with salt and pepper, and place in a shallow dish.

Sauté onion in hot oil until tender.

Add wine, brandy, and herbs.

Pour mixture over steaks; cover and marinate in refrigerator 8 hours.

Drain steaks, reserving marinade.

Sauté steaks in 1 tablespoon butter in a skillet just until lightly browned on both sides.

Place steaks in dish; cover and refrigerate 2 hours.

Meanwhile prepare Spinach Stuffing.

Spinach Stuffing

- 3 tablespoons extra-virgin olive oil
- 1 pound frozen chopped spinach
- 4 cloves garlic, chopped
- 1 to 2 teaspoons red pepper flakes
- ½ cup sweet sherry
- 1 cup fresh bread crumbs
- ½ cup grated Romano cheese
- Salt and freshly ground black pepper
- 1 teaspoon chopped fresh basil leaves
- 1 teaspoon chopped fresh parsley leaves
- 1 teaspoon chopped fresh chives
- 1 teaspoon chopped fresh rosemary leaves
- 1 teaspoon chopped fresh thyme leaves

Cover and chill at least 2 hours.

Roll pastry into an 18-inch square on a lightly floured surface; cut into 6 9x6-inch rectangles.

Spread center of each pastry rectangle with ⅓ cup Spinach Stuffing; top with a steak.

Combine egg yolks and water; brush edges of pastry with mixture.

Fold pastry over, and pinch edges and ends together.

Place Wellingtons, seam side down, on a lightly greased baking sheet.

Brush with egg mixture.

Bake at 400 for 25 minutes or until golden brown.

Combine reserved marinade, beef broth, and tomato paste in a saucepan; cook over medium heat 25 minutes.

Combine cornstarch and Madeira; stir into broth mixture and cook, stirring constantly, until thickened.

Top each Wellington with ¼ cup Madeira sauce to serve.

Bridget's Chocolate Truffles

- 8 ounces of semi-sweet or bittersweet high quality chocolate, chopped into small pieces
- ½ cup heavy whipping cream
- 1 teaspoon pure vanilla extract
- 2 tablespoons amaretto
- 1 teaspoon almond extract
- ½-1 cup cocoa powder for coating

In a saucepan over low heat bring the heavy whipping cream to a simmer.

Place the chocolate in a separate bowl. Pour the cream over the chocolate, add the vanilla, amaretto and almond extract and allow to stand for a few minutes. Stir until smooth. Allow to cool, and place in the refrigerator for 2 hours.

Remove from refrigerator and with a teaspoon roll out balls of the chocolate mixture. Dust your hands with confectioner's sugar to prevent sticking, and roll between your palms quickly to form balls. Place on a baking sheet lined with parchment paper. Place in the refrigerator overnight.

Roll in cocoa powder and serve.

Makes 30-40 chocolate truffles.

Peppermint Cream

- 1 cup heavy whipping cream
- 3 tablespoons confectioners' sugar
- ½ teaspoon peppermint extract
- 6 hard peppermint candies, crushed

In a chilled small mixing bowl and with chilled beaters, beat cream until it begins to thicken. Add confectioners' sugar and peppermint extract; beat until hard peaks form. Stir in crushed peppermint candies. Red food coloring may be added for a festive touch. Store in the refrigerator.

Maryland Crab Cakes
with Remoulade Sauce

- 1 pound fresh lump crabmeat
- 1½ tablespoons dry bread crumbs
- 2 teaspoons chopped fresh parsley
- Salt and pepper to taste
- 1 egg
- 1½ tablespoons mayonnaise
- ½ teaspoon ground dry mustard
- 1 teaspoon Worcestershire sauce
- 2 tablespoons butter

Mix together crabmeat, bread crumbs, parsley, salt and pepper.

Beat together egg, mayonnaise, Worcestershire sauce and mustard. Combine with other ingredients and mix well. Form into 6 large patties or 12-18 small ones.

Melt butter in a heavy skillet. Fry crab cakes until a brown crust forms on each side, about 4 minutes for regular sized cakes.

Serve hot with remoulade sauce (recipe follows).

Remoulade Sauce

- 1 cup mayonnaise
- 2 tablespoons lemon juice
- ½ cup chopped onion
- 2 tablespoons chopped garlic
- 2 tablespoons prepared horseradish
- 3 tablespoons prepared whole-grain mustard
- 2 tablespoons Worcestershire sauce
- 3 tablespoons ketchup
- 1 teaspoon salt
- ¼ teaspoon cayenne pepper
- ⅛ teaspoon freshly ground black pepper

Combine all ingredients in a blender and process until smooth.

Asparagus Casserole

- 2 tablespoons butter, melted
- 12 spears fresh asparagus
- 2 tablespoons onion, diced
- ¼ cup parmesan cheese
- ½ cup bread crumbs
- ½ teaspoon salt
- ⅛ teaspoon pepper
- ¼ teaspoon thyme
- 2 tablespoons sherry

Boil asparagus in boiling water for 3 minutes. Drain well and pat dry.

Pour butter into shallow baking dish. Line bottom with asparagus spears. Mix remaining ingredients together and spread over spears. Cover and bake at 375 for 30-35 minutes or until asparagus is tender.

Broccoli Quiche

- 1 9-inch pie shell
- 2 cups chopped fresh broccoli
- 1 cup thinly sliced fresh mushrooms
- ½ cup milk
- ½ cup heavy cream
- 3 eggs, beaten
- 2 tablespoons butter, melted
- 1 tablespoon flour
- 1 teaspoon salt
- ½ teaspoon pepper
- 1 teaspoon dry mustard
- 1 cup shredded cheddar cheese, divided
- ½ cup asiago grated cheese
- ½ cup mozzarella cheese

Preheat oven to 375. Bake pie crust about 10 minutes or until bottom is slightly brown. Let cool. Cook broccoli until tender; drain well. Combine milk, eggs, butter, flour, salt, pepper and ¾ cup cheese; whisk until well blended. Sprinkle remaining ¼ cup of cheese over crust. Layer broccoli and mushrooms on cheese. Pour milk and egg mixture over all. Bake at 375 for 35 to 45 minutes or until a knife inserted in center comes out clean.

Six Layer Cheese Torte

- 2½ pounds cream cheese
- ½ pound goat cheese
- 1 tablespoon roasted garlic
- ½ cup roasted red pepper pesto
- ½ cup basil pesto
- ½ cup sun dried tomato pesto
- Toasted pine nuts, for garnish

Mix cream cheese, goat cheese, and garlic together. Line a round, greased bowl with plastic wrap. Spray the plastic wrap with non-stick cooking spray. Layer as follows:

⅓ cheese mixture
½ cup red pepper pesto
⅓ cheese mixture
½ cup basil pesto
⅓ cheese mixture
½ cup sun dried tomato pesto

Put in the refrigerator for 4 hours, then unmold onto a serving platter and remove plastic wrap. Sprinkle with toasted pine nuts for garnish.

Tomato Tarts with Black Olives

- 1 dozen prepared individual tart crusts
- 3 medium tomatoes, peeled
- 3 tablespoons finely chopped thyme
- 6 ounces feta cheese (for a different flavor, you may use ¾ cup shredded sharp cheddar)
- ¾ cup chopped black olives
- 2 tablespoons prepared Dijon mustard

Preheat oven to 350.

Slice the tomatoes, sprinkle with salt; remove moisture by pressing them between a stack of paper towels, and covering them with a heavy object (like an iron skillet) for 30 minutes.

Brush the bottoms of each tart with prepared mustard. Dice the tomatoes. Fill each tart halfway full with diced tomatoes, sprinkle with salt and thyme. Crumble cheese on top of tomatoes, top generously with chopped black olives. Bake at 350 20-25 minutes.

Swiss Chard and Goat Cheese Tart

- 1 9-inch pie crust
- 2 tablespoons chopped fresh rosemary
- 1 teaspoon olive oil
- 6 slices bacon
- 2 scallions, chopped
- 1 bunch Swiss chard (leaves only)
- 8 ounces goat cheese

Preheat oven to 350.

Rub the pie crust with olive oil and sprinkle with chopped rosemary.

Fry 6 slices of bacon; remove and crumble.

In the bacon fat, sauté scallions and chard leaves until chard is wilted.

Place the chard mixture in the prepared pie crust. Top with crumbled goat cheese. Top with bacon.

Bake at 350 for 30 minutes or until bubbly.

Ida Mae's Fruitcake

- 2 (8 ounce) containers candied cherries
- 1 (8 ounce) container candied mixed citrus peel
- 2 cups raisins
- 1 cup dried currants
- 1 cup dates, pitted and chopped
- 2 (8 ounce) packages pecans
- ½ cup brandy
- 2½ cups all-purpose flour
- ½ teaspoon baking soda
- 1 teaspoon ground cloves
- 1 teaspoon ground allspice
- 1 teaspoon ground cinnamon
- ½ teaspoon salt
- 1 cup butter
- 2 cups packed brown sugar
- 6 eggs
- 1 cup molasses
- 1 cup grape juice
- 1 bottle good red wine for marinating

In a medium bowl, combine cherries, citrus peel, raisins, currants, dates, and nuts. Stir in brandy; let stand 2 hours, or overnight. Dredge soaked fruit with ½ cup flour.

Preheat oven to 275. Grease a tube pan, line with parchment paper and grease again. In a medium bowl, mix together 2 cups flour, baking soda, cloves, allspice, cinnamon, and salt; set aside.

In a large bowl, cream butter until light. Gradually blend in brown sugar and eggs. Mix together molasses and grape juice. Beat into butter mixture alternately with flour mixture, making 4 dry and 3 liquid additions. Fold in floured fruit. Turn into prepared pan.

Bake in preheated oven for 3 to 3½ hours, or until a toothpick inserted into the center of cake comes out clean. Remove from pan, and lift off paper. Cool cake completely. Pour ½ cup wine over the cake and wrap tightly in a cloth towel, then cover with wax paper.

Pour ½ cup wine over the cake each week until wine is gone, wrapping tightly again after each pouring.

Fruitcake should marinate at least 4 weeks, and should be started at Thanksgiving to serve by Christmas.

Ida Mae's Fruitcake Cookies

- 1 cup butter
- 2 cups packed dark brown sugar
- 1 cup white sugar
- 4 eggs
- 1 teaspoon vanilla
- 1 pound chopped dates
- 2 pounds candied fruit
- 1 cup fruit brandy, bourbon, or spirit of choice
- 2 tablespoons milk
- 4 cups flour
- 1 teaspoon soda
- 1 teaspoon salt
- 1 teaspoon ground cinnamon
- 1 teaspoon nutmeg
- ½ teaspoon allspice
- ¼ teaspoon ginger
- ¼ teaspoon cloves
- 2 pounds chopped walnuts

Cream together butter, sugar, vanilla and eggs. Beat in brandy and milk. In a separate bowl, dredge the candied fruit and dates in one cup flour. To the creamed mixture, gradually add the remaining flour and spices. Stir in dredged fruit and nuts. Refrigerate overnight.

Preheat oven to 350. Drop mixture by tea-spoonfuls, approximately 2 inches apart, onto ungreased cookie sheet. Bake 10-12 minutes or until golden on the bottom. Cookies should be chewy. Cool on wire racks.

Makes approximately 4 dozen. Store in tightly concealed container in a cool place for up to a month.

Ladybug Cookies

- 1 cup butter
- 1 cup sugar
- 2 eggs
- 1 teaspoon peppermint extract
- 1½ cups baking flour
- 1 teaspoon baking powder
- 1 teaspoon salt
- Red food coloring (optional)

Preheat oven to 350.

Mix first 4 ingredients. Add dry ingredients a little at a time. Add red food coloring until the dough is a bright red shade.

Cover and refrigerate at least one hour. Roll out ¼-inch thick on floured surface. Cut into circles with a cookie cutter dipped in flour and place on ungreased cookie sheet. Roll ¼ teaspoon of dough into a small ball for each cookie, then flatten and attach the ladybug "head." (This is a great job for children, who can shape the head of each ladybug and give it personality.) Bake 8 minutes on ungreased cookie sheet until light golden. Cool and decorate with butter cream frosting (recipe follows).

Buttercream Frosting
- 3 cups confectioners' sugar
- 1 stick butter, softened
- 2-4 tablespoons milk
- 1 teaspoon almond flavoring
- Red food coloring

Beat softened butter with almond flavoring until fluffy. Add confectioners' sugar, one cup at a time, and beat until smooth. Add milk, one tablespoon at a time, until frosting is of spreading consistency. Add food coloring until a nice shade of red is obtained.

Decorations:
- 1 bag semi-sweet chocolate chips
- Red Decorator's Sugar

Melt ½ bag chocolate chips in a double boiler until smooth. Dip the "heads" of each ladybug into the chocolate and place on wax paper to set.

Frost the body of the ladybug with red buttercream frosting.

While frosting is wet, sprinkle liberally with red sugar (or dip the cookie in a plate of red sugar and shake off the excess).

Place chocolate chips on the body of the cookie for the ladybug's spots.

Bridget's Best-Ever Cookies

- 1 cup butter, softened
- ¾ cup packed light brown sugar
- ½ cup white sugar
- 2 eggs
- ½ teaspoon vanilla extract
- ½ teaspoon almond extract
- 2½ cups all-purpose flour
- 1 teaspoon baking soda
- ½ teaspoon salt
- ½ cup coarsely chopped pecans
- ¾ cup white chocolate chips
- ½ cup butterscotch chips

Preheat oven to 350.

In a large bowl, cream together the butter, brown sugar, and white sugar until smooth. Beat in the eggs, one at a time, then stir in the vanilla and almond extracts. Combine the flour, baking soda, and salt; gradually stir into the creamed mixture. Stir in the nuts, white chocolate chips and butterscotch chips. Drop dough by teaspoonfuls onto ungreased cookie sheets.

Bake for 10 minutes in the preheated oven, or until golden brown.

Ida Mae's Chocolate Chocolate Chip Cookies

- 1 cup butter, softened
- 1½ cups white sugar
- 2 eggs
- 2 teaspoons vanilla extract
- 2¼ cups all-purpose flour
- ½ cup cocoa powder
- ¾ teaspoon baking soda
- ¼ teaspoon salt
- 1 cup semi-sweet chocolate chips
- 1 cup white chocolate chips
- ½ cup chopped walnuts (optional)

Preheat oven to 350.

In large bowl, beat butter, sugar, eggs, and vanilla until light and fluffy. Combine the flour, cocoa, baking soda, and salt; stir into the butter mixture until well blended. Mix in the chocolate chips, white chocolate chips and walnuts. Drop by rounded teaspoonfuls onto ungreased cookie sheets.

Bake for 8 to 10 minutes in the preheated oven, or just until set. Cool slightly on the cookie sheets before transferring to wire racks to cool completely.

Derrick's Southern Comfort Eggnog

Purists may object, but using ice cream instead of raw eggs allows this eggnog to travel well for holiday parties and eliminates concerns about unpasteurized dairy products.

- 1 pound superfine sugar
- 1 cup Southern Comfort liqueur
- ¼ cup rum
- ¼ cup bourbon
- ½ gallon high-quality vanilla ice cream
- 1 quart heavy cream
- 1 tablespoon nutmeg plus more for garnish

Let ice cream melt in a large bowl overnight.

In a separate bowl, stir together sugar, Southern Comfort, rum and bourbon until dissolved. Add cream. Add melted ice cream and nutmeg, and whip with mixer until well blended.

Pour into punch bowl or large pitcher and garnish with nutmeg. Serve chilled.

About the Author

Donna Ball is the author of over a hundred novels under several different pseudonyms in a variety of genres that include romance, mystery, suspense, paranormal, western adventure, historical and women's fiction. Recent popular series include the Ladybug Farm series by Berkley Books and the Raine Stockton Dog Mystery series. She lives in a restored Victorian barn in the heart of the Blue Ridge mountains with a variety of four-footed companions. You can contact her at http://www.donnaball.net

Center Point Large Print
600 Brooks Road / PO Box 1
Thorndike ME 04986-0001 USA

(207) 568-3717

US & Canada:
1 800 929-9108
www.centerpointlargeprint.com